CATALOGUE:
A MENU OF MEMORIES

CATALOGUE:
A MENU OF MEMORIES

RAVI TEJA

PARTRIDGE

Copyright © 2016 by RAVI TEJA.

ISBN: Softcover   978-1-4828-7039-8
              eBook   978-1-4828-7038-1

Because of the dynamic nature of the Internet, any web addresses or links contained in this book may have changed since publication and may no longer be valid. The views expressed in this work are solely those of the author and do not necessarily reflect the views of the publisher, and the publisher hereby disclaims any responsibility for them.

Print information available on the last page.

To order additional copies of this book, contact
Partridge India
000 800 10062 62
orders.india@partridgepublishing.com

www.partridgepublishing.com/india

"This anthology is dedicated to all of its contributors"

&

Editing Credits

Special Thanks to Shamita Harsh and Shreyasi Phukon

CONTENTS

Shamita Harsh

Shamita Harsh (Born on 23rd August 1993) is an author at heart, a graduate of Mass communication, a freelance columnist by profession. Up until now she had lived all her life with her parents in Dehradun, the tinsel town she grew up in. She has now moved to Delhi. She is currently pursuing her MA in Convergent Journalism at Jamia's AJKMCRC department. Her first step into the writing kingdom was with her debut novel that was published at the age of 19. The story is a journey of friendship of five very unique girls: The Creepy Cuties. Finally the 5 girls of Creepy Cuties found their way out of the closet with the dream of a writer in tow! The Creepy Cuties is a novel of the young adult fiction genre.

Her more recent conquests are:

- Ella's only Story (a modern day fairy tale with magical realism as its central theme) published in I an Anthology of Short Stories by FirstStep Publishers, and
- My Shadow self (a writer's struggle between her real identity and the one that is conjured up in her dreams), another short story in a thriller anthology called Once Upon a Time, to be published by Sanmati publishers this September.

A born writer at heart, she owes it to her father for the lineage of writing and for the inkling toward the creative! In her spare time she likes to pen her thoughts and poems in her journal, a prized possession she keeps ever since she was 11. A right-brained thinker, Shamita loves to write fiction triggered from observing nuances of life around her. A devoted reader, she hordes books for pleasure in her tiny shoe-rack-turned-into-a-library.

"For me, friendship is the happy connection that oils the rusty wheel of life. One advice for anyone and everyone, if you believe (enough) YOU can make your dreams happen, just like I did!"- Shamita

1

PAINT ME MY MEMORIES

Shamita Harsh

I have a memory, one not very clear, because with time it tends to fade or just become even clearer. I feel it depends on the person you relate the memory with. If deep down you don't want to keep the memory, it fades away quicker than others. And others you wish to keep close to your heart until your memory itself begins to fade away like words on a letter stored for several years.

"The Dehradun platform is slowly left behind and the objects on it diminish in size until they are nothing but tiny freckles. The mango trees are whizzing by as the train is gaining momentum. The concrete has devoured even the outskirts of what once had been our cozy town." Ruchi told Simmi.

Two girls sat in a train compartment, eager for the journey. One was small, cute and had a grace that would only fit an artist. Ruchi had her arm tucked into her friend's. The other was taller, with sharper features and was agile with her long strides. Simmi had eyes that remained lowered for some reason.

Simmi had that look on her face, the one she got when an adventure was going to begin in her head. She said, "See there that old lady glides on top of the train roof in her white gown and her long cascading hair. She sings a song of misery."

"Oh I can see her now!" Ruchi exclaimed. "I can see her waltzing on the train-top. She's not really walking on the train; she's just sort of hovering…"

Simmi continued, "And she just sort of floats up to our window and materializes besides us."

Ruchi carried on, "She's the old lady from our memories alright. She's the one we saw at the Haunted House. She's the one who has been watching over us all along. I think …I think…I think…"

Simmi finished off for her, "I think she's our Godmother or perhaps our Guardian Angel."

To some, it seemed like nonsensical conversation, but to these two girls this was normal routine. They would imagine things, picture them, and then describe it to each other. They took lead from each other's ideas, spinning tales in their wake. It was like plotting a memory to keep, an idea to preserve.

Simmi was an author and Ruchi was an artist. The two girls had been best friends ever since they had been in diapers. This had been their tale of friendship. Though they had only known each other for 4 years, the girls liked to believe that their friendship had begun the moment they had been born. It was the way they connected their stories. It was the way they lived happily ever after. Each of them had been lonely in their childhood and they just clicked so perfectly in college that they felt like they had known each other since forever. So they didn't have any memories of their past together, not the recent past, but the one they had left behind, the one in which they didn't have each other. To compensate for all those years, they created memories and in those memories they created a childhood, a high school, a neighborhood, a common market place and everything they would have had together when they were younger. And in that world Simmi wrote stories from those memories and Ruchi painted pictures.

"I have a memory Ruchi. One I'd like to write about. Will you paint it for me?"

"Sure sweety. Which one is it?" Ruchi implored. But she already knew the answer as she drew out her notepad from the bag.

Their memories were connected. The two girls shared a space in each others' brains. The sheer concept was laughable, sharing memories in such a way, but those who had witnessed them vouched for it. The girls knew each others' heart back and front. They could conjure up a dream and make the other one envision it. They could finish off each other's sentences, thoughts, ideas; you name it. They knew each other so well that they could practically read each other's minds.

Simmi began with a voice not less poignant than a story-teller's, "It's us on the bridge..."

"... Where we were looking at fishes in the little stream, and you dropped your favorite pen in the water." Ruchi completed.

Simmi smiled as if she could still picture the day clearly. She went on, "I remember I couldn't stop wailing for the stupid pen, but you see it was the one..."

"...Your grandfather had given to you. And you couldn't bear to part with it." Ruchi could feel her throat constricting as she began to sketch the details of that memory.

Simmi laughed as the image swam before her eyes, "And you being the great friend you have always been, jumped into the stream, even though you didn't know how to swim!"

Ruchi joined her in the mirth but her thoughts were elsewhere. Memories: fresh or stale. But unfortunately, her friend only had old memories to live by; she couldn't create new ones, or rather had no recent ones.

If only she hadn't been so stubborn that night. Ruchi drifted off to another memory, this one harsher than the strokes of the one she drew on the paper.

Simmi realized Ruchi had stopped sketching much before her pencil really stopped. She knew better than to question her friend. She also knew that guilt hung in the stale air of the train cabin.

Simmi had all but tried to convince Ruchi that nothing was her fault but she blamed herself nonetheless. She had told her countless times that it could have happened with anybody, but to no effect. It was the only malady she couldn't cure in her friend's heart.

It had been almost a week since they hadn't met or spoken to each other. I am not going to take the blame this time, Ruchi remembered telling herself over and over again. How could her friend be so self-centered? She hadn't called once. Okay, so her other friends had come into town and they had gone out but that didn't mean Sim would just forget about her. She could have asked her for that movie. Sim had known she had been dying to see it in the theatre!

But well the matter hadn't been that petty. The problems in their friendship had longer roots and sitting in the train compartment Ruchi found herself going though those memories. Snapshots of their lives, which weren't as happy as the others, mounted on a high-speed roll film. It made the scenes play before her eyes like rushed montages trying to show her everything but in a short span of time.

Simmi tuned her thoughts in like a radio trying to catch a frequency. She could almost sense the pattern of Ruchi's memories as they whizzed by her.

Simmi had been struggling since college to get published and when her first manuscript had been accepted, nobody could have been happier than her oldest friend.

Ruchi had been there by her side to support her through thick and thin. But Simmi had become too busy to notice that Ruchi also had a life of her own.

The day the Author Copies had arrived at Simmi's place she had wanted to go, but something had come up. That didn't mean she was less of a friend.

And then only a few days later Simmi had lost her grandfather. Ruchi had been too busy with her papers or else she would have never left her closest friend to cry alone that night. If it would have been for her, she would have been the shoulder Simmi wept at the day of the funeral.

That was the first time her friendship with Simmi left a bitter after-taste in her mouth.

Simmi had begun to notice the selfish-streaks and realized she had been selfish. The selfish days of her working on her books; snapping at her like that just because she was in between the moods that were only typical to an author, when Ruchi had only been trying to help. The path to friendship was a two-way street and the cracks in their friendship had been two-fold as well.

When they had had a connection as pure as theirs, there would be certainly a good deal of memories to share. But Simmi had begun to feel suffocated by their memories. Ruchi was always conjuring up their childhood dreams or their high school ones. Though they were certainly special, Simmi just needed a break. She needed to create new memories and so she had begun to drift away.

Simmi found herself thinking the way she had back then. The memory of like-minded thoughts, thoughts you had had some time ago, that gave you a sense of déjà vu.

It began to take shape in her mind: I liked to pretend I was a statue. The world could just go by admiring me, but never really seeing me. And as for me, I would sit there in a regal posture seeing and hearing all that went beneath the layers of practiced façade. I would not only watch but see that couple had issues they weren't ready to say out loud. I could hear and not just listen the hidden meaning of fake formalities. If I could watch people living their lives; rushing from one task to another, ticking off things in their mental To-do Lists of the day; always having an agenda and never really stopping to breathe, never really stopping to enjoy life as they led them.

So I went to the park each evening, and I could witness the world in a slightly more relaxed atmosphere. I would sit beside the fountain, that had long stopped working and I would watch a movie. Not the reel variety but the real kind. And so for that one hour every day, I would soak in memories that others created. Memories that were not my own, but I took them in nonetheless. Because these were the slices of life I learnt from. The glimpse of that sad widow walking alone in the park, of that couple yelling profanities over whose turn was it to change the diaper in the midst of the park or perhaps that lost soul who wandered the dark alleys at night.

If Ruchi would have been with her she would have sketched the scene right out of her head. She was truly talented and the strokes of her work never failed to amaze her.

Ruchi had noticed her sitting there only too often. She knew that the place brought peace in her life. Simmi had been blessed with a great family but she always felt something was missing and Ruchi seemed to complete that circle for her. The vicious circle of memories could be lethal, like a merry-go-round spinning on top speed. It would become difficult to step out of that and even when you found an escape you would be left with a nauseous feeling. The circle of Simmi's memories, these memories would have faded up until recently if it hadn't been for Ruchi.

What is a writer but a great observer of the past, who transforms memories into words! They might be his they might be another's but they are memoirs of someone's life alright. Ruchi had noticed her friend's talent from almost day one of college. Her ability to spin words into a lore so exciting, you could barely sit straight, never failed to amaze her.

That night Simmi had decided to make amends. Not talking to her best friend had only made life miserable. With their parents back home, they only had each other in the city. Always the peacemaker, Simmi had found herself thinking. Over the years she had always been the one who broke the ice, always the one who took the first step to sort things out.

But perhaps not this time, she thought as she struggled to make a decision. With a hand on the doorknob she glanced at the window. From her first-floor apartment she could see the beginnings of a storm were brewing in the atmosphere. Winds seemed stronger as if gearing up for the night. Great, that was just great!

One look at her wristwatch told her it was nearing 8 o'clock. Darkness had already enveloped the night. Maybe she should call to check if she was home. It was Thursday night; Ruchi would have probably gotten home late from work and was sitting in front of her T.V. eating take-out.

She took the steps and as she made her way out of her building she dialed Ruchi's number. The cell phone rang out of rings but she didn't pick up. Thinking she might have been in the washroom, Simmi redialed, sending a mute prayer along. This time she picked up on the 3rd ring.

"Hello?" Ruchi said in a clipped voice.

Simmi sighed; she shouldn't have called. Ruchi's voice clearly told her she was in no mood to talk. But then her pride wouldn't be the one to sort this fight.

"Hi Ginty, how are you?" Simmi managed in her most cheery voice, using Ruchi's pet name that she had coined, to soften her.

"Fine. What about you?" Ruchi had replied curtly. This was the thing with her; she always became too negative during a fight and began to take all things in the wrong sense. Once someone got on her wrong side, they would pretty much stay there. Simmi had witnessed this over the years and she also knew try as she might, this Ice Princess was hard to melt.

"I'm good and I'm on my way over..." Simmi ventured.

She heard the audible sigh of frustration and glanced around the pavement. Ruchi's apartment was only a couple of blocks away. The storm was gaining momentum. Trees had begun to sway. There was light traffic on the road. She decided to wait just a bit longer and reason with her friend over the phone. That way she could put a chink in the wall her friend had built between them.

"Please don't," Ruchi said on the other end, "I don't want to see you right now. How hard is it to wrap your brain around that?"

The blow hit her hard. But Simmi knew enough, not to take it to the heart. She was used to listening to such hurtful things once Ruchi got into a temper. She knew her friend only tried to push people out with that trick; knew it too well. She knew it because until a little while ago, she had been the same way.

Simmi closed her eyes, took a deep breath and tried sending happy memories in Ruchi's direction. She gulped, trying to fight back the sting in her eyes as tears threatened on their corners.

When careless thoughts take shape into memories, they usually conjure up images of what we are thinking.

Ruchi sat on the couch before her television set, eating take-out. And in that moment of silence she pictured Simmi's beautiful eyes filled with hurt. Immediately she chided herself for the horrible treatment she had been giving her friend. She didn't deserve it. She wished she hadn't wasted a whole week not talking to her, sending her angry messages and ignoring her calls. God, she had been rude.

Ruchi had had a picture before her, as real as any reality, yet she knew it was only a memory. God forbid, if something were to happen to Simmi, something like an accident, what would Ruchi remember as the last memory she had shared with her. She would stand between her friend and whatever it was that tried to harm her. She remembered feeling guilty to think of such a bad omen, but she couldn't help but see the error of her ways.

She was all but ready to apologize as she opened her eyes.

Simmi opened hers at the same time.

The next thing she knew, Ruchi heard a loud crash.

The next thing she knew, Simmi saw shards of glass flying towards her. She tried to shield herself but it was too late.

An accident, Ruchi wasn't just dreaming. There had been an accident and Simmi was hurt. She could feel it. She yelled into the phone, "SIMMMMMMMMMMMMMIIIIIIIIIIII…!"

But the line had already disconnected as Simmi had fallen on the ground, her cell-phone with her.

Her last conscious memory was Ruchi's face. Only a memory, she couldn't even see her friend one last time.

What is a memory but a piece of our lives tucked away in the bone-china cabinets of our hearts or perhaps locked away in the dark dungeons, waiting to come out at the happy occasion or the depressed one.

The memory which came to her now was a sad one. Ruchi could feel it happening all over again in the train compartment.

Ruchi ran the two blocks, with the wind howling in her ears. She had goosebumps on her skin. As she rounded the corner, panting, she saw the truck.

Shards of glass lay strewn on the road. Ruchi knew she didn't want this memory in her head, but she had to see her friend. She made her way around the truck to see her lying there. Her feet came into view first and Ruchi slowly completed the turn seeing her knees, her stomach, her hands, her neck, scanning her body. She observed no damage there as she scanned her body from toe to head, until she saw her eyes. They were closed but they were bleeding.

Bleeding, so profusely, her baby, her friend, the only person she cared for. She didn't remember how long she stood there, but the sirens from the ambulance were her bugle to sprint into action.

She lifted her in her arms, heavy, as it was she didn't care. She wasn't going to leave her body aside. She hauled her friend into the ambulance and yelled at the driver, "Move it!"

Her next memory was perhaps even worse than finding your best friends body immobile on the footpath. She sat outside the I.C.U. waiting and praying. She had never believed in God. Simmi had been the religious one, the faithful believer that everything happened for a reason and God had a hand in every success of her life. But Ruchi had never really understood her faith. Today, however, was a different story. So she begged to Simmi's God to keep her friend alive.

The pages in Ruchi's mind turned. This one was a memory when the inspector in charge of the case had walked up to her. From her miserable heap on the floor, she had looked up to see bright intelligent eyes.

He spoke to her, "Ruchi Rai? Friend of Simmi Harsh? May I have a word with you?"

She nodded, having lost all energy to speak.

"This is regarding the accident," he began, "Your friend was standing on the curb off Vasant Vihar, facing the main Highway. She was apparently speaking on the phone and we traced the last call of her sim-card to your number. At 8:07pm a truck on the highway narrowly missed a car and swerved off the main road. The driver managed to put a break but the tires skidded off the road, onto the curb and halted as they hit a lamp post. Your friend was standing there, perhaps unaware of the accident, right beneath the lamp post on the curb…"

Ruchi tuned out the rest of it. She realized Simmi's eyes had been closed because she had just heard some mean words from her closest friend. So obviously she hadn't seen the approaching truck. Thankfully the truck never touched her. It was the moment Ruchi remembered envisioning the accident.

Sitting beside her friend in the train she realized God had heard her prayer, if only she had made a more full-proof prayer request to the Almighty that night. She was still thankful to have her, he had indeed made Ruchi's shield between her friend and any harm she might have come to. Simmi had emerged unscathed for most part of the accident, the truck hadn't been able to cause any harm.

The curb, the edge of the pavement, where Simmi always stood on to make her calls before crossing the road. Her friend had always said, "It's downright dangerous to talk on this devil device as you drive let alone as you walk on the road, one distraction…and…"

"And boom…!" Ruchi remembered finishing off her thought.

The doctor walked out of the I. C. U. and she turned her attention to him. He met her expectant eyes, "The patient had pieces of a broken tube-light in her eyes along with some shards of glass when she was brought in. We were successful in taking out all the pieces but I am afraid her eyes… The surgery…"

All Ruchi really remembered in that memory was the doctor speaking a lot of technical nonsense, until she yelled, "Tell me what's wrong in simple words. I am not a doctor and I sucked at Biology in school, just tell me what's wrong with her?"

The hospital staff had looked at her with anxious glances. Perplexed the doctor had explained.

Ruchi didn't remember sitting on the floor with a thump with a head over her mouth so that the hospital won't be disturbed by her screams.

This one memory had no pictures for Simmi. She had woken up from what seemed like a long slumber. She had opened her eyes and then there was nothing. She had been confused because she didn't remember where she was and she couldn't see anything around her. Maybe she was in a dream she thought, because this surely couldn't have been a memory.

Ruchi had spoken from somewhere close by then, "Hi Sim. How are you feeling?"

"I…I'm …what's wrong Ruchi? What happened? Where am I?" she stammered as her mind tried to locate a memory, any memory. But all she could find was darkness. She searched and searched but her mind came up with dead ends alone.

In soothing tones, Ruchi explained the accident. She reached the end without really telling her the truth. She looked around in her friend's hospital room. The nurse on duty smiled sympathetically.

"Simmi, baby, Oh God, how do I …okay…sim…listen… umm…the accident…" Ruchi managed to blurt out.

For a moment there was silence. Simmi felt like she skipped a heartbeat. What? As reality sank in, she broke into sobs.

That night Ruchi remembered was a painful memory they had created together. They lay cuddled on Simmi's hospital bed. Ruchi hugging her friend from behind as both of them cried into the night.

Ruchi woke up with a jolt.

Simmi, sensing her friend awake, offered her one ear-plug of the headphones she was listening music in. Ruchi gladly accepted it, and they both bowed their heads in as if this was a practiced habit of theirs. The song was 'Let It Go' from the new Frozen movie.

They found themselves sharing memories again. There is always that beautiful song that sets off memories in your heart. The lyrics are so good that you feel that the song was written for you.

"Oh look," Ruchi cried out. The train had stopped at a platform and Ruchi picked up the next subject for their memory. She sang out to her friend, "There is a tree just outside the platform. One of the branches look like a witch mounted on her broomstick."

Simmi laughed at her friend's voice that was befitting a musical. "You paint that Ginty! I wanna see it too. I am sure this wicked witch is cackling at all the miserable souls in this compartment!"

That got them both started again. They laughed between their ideas and sang their sentences, painting beautiful pictures in their mind's eye. These were the best sort of memories, the ones which had no photographic proof whatsoever but were so deeply ingrained in their hearts that they felt real.

The charms bracelet caught her eye. It was all but glittering in the sun. Ruchi had seen it a million times; she had a similar one on her wrist as well. But still the words seemed to beckon to her each time she thought about Simmi. The beauty of the bracelet never failed to amaze her. It had been Simmi's idea, who else could have described their friendship in a better way.

Ruchi understood it now, by the time notes of the song faded away, she had made peace with the guilt. She understood it now. She couldn't blame herself for the accident just like you couldn't blame a victim. As the sun shone her friend's ebony black hair she understood the reason for their link, their memories. She felt a heavy weight lift off her heart.

"Thank you for the memories," Ruchi murmured in her best friend's ear.

MEMORIES, the charms read, each charm designed for each letter. The links that bound the charms together were the the memories that had bound them together.

Knowing what her friend meant, Simmi traced the letters on her hand and smiled in gleeful abandon.

Everyone questioned themselves at one point or the other, but the girls had risen above the misunderstandings that had been nothing but gaps in communication and found the true meaning of magical friendship.

The other passengers in their coach were wary by now. It was a long ride from Dehradun to Mumbai by train and the passengers weren't in their most comfortable of seats, nor were they in their happiest of moods.

Some looked irritated by the constant chitter-chatter. Some tried to eavesdrop and were amazed. Some even smirked. What lunatics, they thought to themselves, staring or exchanging disbelieving looks!

They didn't know Ruchi took care of Simmi in away her parents couldn't. They didn't know that these descriptions were sketched by Ruchi on Braille sheets. They didn't know that Simmi did remember the places of every letter on the QWERTY keyboard and so she could still type her stories most of them, but Ruchi proofed them, just in case. They didn't know that this was the method they had coordinated to keep Simmi's dreams alive. They didn't know that Ruchi drew the book covers on Simmi's books and had devoted her life for her friend's dreams, not out of guilt but for compassion. They didn't know that once the ideas were created they lived in a carefree way tackling hardships together; creating wonderful memories, anyone else would have given up. They didn't know that this Braille system was the means through which Simmi could "see" the paintings.

They didn't know Simmi was blind.

There is magic in our memories, we can conjure up any part of the spells we wish to brew.

Pranav Shree

Pranav Shree, 20, is a fourth engineering student at Lovely Professional University. While pursuing his engineering degree, he has made a name in freelancing world and has received job offers from various native and foreign publishing houses and writing firms. He has contributed a short story in the anthology—A Phase Unknown-Woman A Tribute. His writing has been acclaimed by national daily Hindustan Times and his articles are regularly featured in his university's newspaper.

He believes that the youth of contemporary India is very talented but misdirected, he wants to help them realize their field of interest and do something grandeur in the same, he has made some strides in the same direction with Gate Counselor.

You can reach him at - pranavshree14@gmail.com

2

TWISTED LOVE

Pranav Shree

"We often do it! Sit and stare incessantly at our recently clicked snaps! What do we really look for? How beautiful we have grown? Or how smartly the photographer has hidden our obscurities and presented a viscous picture of our demons?

We all do it, we do it so often that we lose count and yet we are not satisfied of what we see because instead of being proud about how good we look on screen we are sad about the person we have turned out to be.

We are sad about the so-called-friends we have lost over the course of time and still continue to lose. We are doubtful about our future given the present that seems vague and we stare at ourselves trying to decipher the moments when things went wrong.

The photograph is merely a coordinated presentation of the happenings from the past. When we stare at ourselves we pose questions and all we get to hear in return are excuses coveted under the synonym - The-fault-in-our-stars even though they are-the-faults-in-us.

We continue to live life, as it comes to us and one day when everything seems too different and difficult we feel inferior and we feel lost and all we do is look for answers in our past. It can be anything, the move you made to win your friend back or the simple suggestion you cited to make your friend's life better; if it was love that changed your life then the reason for the mishap can be none other than expectations, because we all believe love to be one-stop-shop for things we dream of, while love is a farm where you need to work through sunny and rainy days to grow the world which you deserve more than the world you need.

The world would have been a better place if we judged less and loved more, the world would have been a far better place if we would have been less envious and more jovial about others success".

Rahul had spent writing for three hours incessantly, he was about to shut his laptop down and surrender himself to the world of dreams, when he received a message on his Facebook account, with drowsy eyes and groggy emotions he switched tabs and read the message, least he knew, that one message will change his life forever.

-x-x-

Love, can we really define it, if yes, then why people fail to recognize true love and are always victimized by the wrong ones.

Rahul was in his second year of engineer and till date all he had experienced in the name of love was naughty make outs, back seat kisses and late night phone sex. Love to Rahul was something, which he had experienced with Payal in X standard, with Visakha in XI standard and with Priyanka in first year of his engineering college. He was not in love at any of those moments with any of those girls, he just thought himself into the idea that he was. He was yet to experience true love.

But then, love comes to those, whose lives are imperfect. Love at times come to make it better while most of the time it completely messes it up.

One such Love story is of Rahul and Heena, set in the most astonishing situation with weird Serendipities... (Finding your Love on Facebook is indeed Serendipity…) Rahul, a college going guy whose physical appearance can be illustrated as scrawny with a bizarre swaging style (lopsided ass), the only thing good about his personality which made girls lose their control over their hearts was his dark complexion, which made him look like a star freshly out into the studio for some action.

While, Heena was a beauty, she had an incomparable fairness with charisma that can put pearls to shame; she was all that a boy like Rahul could dream off. Heena was a cocktail that was going to turn Rahul, tipsy for a lifetime.

x—x—x

It had been a bad day for Rahul, he was sent out of his class because of being sleepy. The only good thing that happened to him that night was the prose he wrote for his innocuous blog; he was hell tired because of the basketball session after class. He planned to retire to bed after completing his daily writing exercise.

Rahul was dreaming of being one of India's most loved writer, he never wanted to sell millions of copies but he wanted to help people realize their dreams and he wanted people to relate themselves to his story and take something good out of it and he was hell bent about his career as a Writer. He had planned his future accordingly; he was all set to make every endeavor to set his life straight as a Writer.

After completing his writing exercise, he migrated towards Facebook to read the one message which arrived recently into his message box.

Heena:-Hii! Rahul, this is Heena from Delhi and I found you on Facebook page of massively huge Lovely Professional University. Actually bored with vacation, I logged into Facebook and saw the comment you left on LPU's page very meticulously (although it comprised of less admiration and more abuses.)The comment intrigued me into your profile and I ended up texting you on Facebook. I fervor you will reply with genuine info and try not to disguise me with delusions and oxymoron statements about your University (am not expecting you as a flirt but the thing is 'most of the boys are flirt and the rest have to suffer', can't help) Signing off ~ Heena...

"Whoa", was the only word Rahul quipped; with scintillating eyes he sat straight on his bed to reply.

Hey Heena! Talking about LPU, makes me feel proud. We do not need to feign pride, it comes naturally. The atmosphere here is exciting and inspiring; administration is supportive too. Being a girl you will find yourself safe within the boundaries of LPU, and yes, if you land in here, do let me know.

P.S:- I am not a flirt, but always available as a Lovelite.

Heena was waiting for his reply; she found his profile picture extremely hot, she liked the way he was smiling in his profile picture. For once she thought of sending an "Add request", but thinking "he might take it in wrong way", she dropped the idea.

Her phone beeped, excitingly she read the message loud to her mom and they both got into laughter after reading the "P.S" part of the text.

Heena's mom ended up saying, "He seems to be a good guy".

Heena smiled and quipped, "Do you think so?"

Her mother quipped 'Yes' with a sense of approval.

Heena smiled and showed her mom Rahul's photos from Facebook. On seeing his photos, her mom was like, "Oh my god, he is so handsome", she even added, "Your dad was the same in his youth, Dark and Handsome".

Heena smiled to his mom. She replied to Rahul's message with full excitement.

"Thanks man, you have really been a great help. Really supportive and not a flirt for sure. I'll definitely let you know, when I reach there."

Rahul was busy with his books; he was adding metaphors to his mind. He read the message and replied with a "☺".

#2 months later…

Summer was fading, Rahul was back to college, a new semester was about to start. He entered his flat and saw the messed up condition in which they had left the flat three months ago. He got into the flat and cleaned it up. It took him three long hours cleaning it, later on; he arranged all the things he brought back from home. Settling down on bed with his MacBook, he logged into Facebook.

Logging into Facebook, he saw a message from Heena, saying, "Thank you".

Rahul with a smile on his spent face, replied with, "So you are in here?"

Heena- Yep…
Rahul- Hmmm, so, did you like it?
Heena- Yeah! It is massively huge.
Rahul- Any friends??

Heena noticed; the number of question marks was increasing with the number of questions. A sign of interest, she considered it as.

Heena- No one, except you ;)
Rahul- ☺
Heena- ☺

Ohkay! Then good night, got a class tomorrow early morning.

Rahul- Ohkay! Good night.
Heena- btw, don't you think, I owe you a treat for being available as a Lovelite.
Rahul- Haha! Sure, tomorrow 4 p.m?
Heena- Ohk! Done. Meet at Architecture building.

He was there, sharply at 4. He took a bit to recognize her, although he had seen her profile pictures.

To Rahul, Heena came out to be more beautiful than her profile picture. He told her, "You are beautiful", she sighed saying, "Thank You".

First meeting was beautiful, two young, beautiful people and a cup of coffee. By the end of the date, Heena was laughing at him and he was getting serious for her. He saw tears in her eyes, while talking about her Ex. Heena was incessantly calling him Nerd and Jerk.

They exchanged their numbers and started talking till wee hours in the morning. She shared everything about her, but Rahul was reluctant to share his past, he feared losing her because of his philandering past. After noticing tears in her eyes while talking about her Exes, he realized that he was the kind of guy that made girls like her cry. He felt bad and weighed by that feeling, he felt a change within himself and he felt love for her.

He was in love with her, outrageously. One night when things between them were a bit serious, he confessed his love to her over the phone.

She smiled and said, "Love is the best feeling, it is even better than the feeling of impediment and success and I too feel the same for you, I love you too…"

-x-x-x-

Rahul was always wooed by her cute little activities; at times she used to imitate his stern tone of speaking; at times she used to keep her head on his shoulder and say nothing; she was the best to Rahul; a cocktail of women Rahul had been with in his past life, Heena was the cocktail served chilled.

Love between them grew, as they grew old together.

One evening, perched comfortably on a concrete bench, hands in hands, Heena out of nowhere, asked Rahul, So, you want to be a Writer???

Rahul, under shock, nodded firmly.

Heena- What you going to write? Love stories???

Rahul- Yep, Love stories, probably ours.

Heena- Ours? What? What in ours to be written, and how will you write.

Rahul, was a true artist, he believed "Art is an anonymous part of reality, Abstract but vague".

He answered Heena in a romantic way, his answer left Heena surprised and astonished.

"If ever I sit down to write a book, I'll start with the day we met… Followed by your character sketch, where I'll define how beautiful you are, I'll make other girls envy you and boys jealous of me…

The next chapter will tell you "how stupid I am" and "how stupidly I love you"…

Turning pages you will realize the intensity of my love and passionate desires...Goose bumps and blushes will be frequent for your body and lips...

Chapters with names like "Breathless" and "Promises" will set new definitions of Love and Romance...Every letter I wrote to you on yellow rusty pages will do the work of awesome poems; people will laugh and cry at the same time reading the story, Mine and Your Story...

If ever I sit down to write a book I'll relive all the moments... Love will be rejuvenated, Moments will come Alive...

If Ever I Sit Down To Write a Book, I'll Love You More Than Ever..."

-x-x-x-

It was their fifth month anniversary, with the euphoric memory and love of five long months Rahul asked his angel Heena to accompany him for a Movie.

Heena stared at him with an inscrutable smile.

Registering a smile on her face, Rahul asked her "is that a Yes".

Heena replied with "Ummm, hmmm", then she leaped over him and gave a soft peck on his lips and then mumbled "that's a Yes".

The lights started fading off as the silver curtain played a series of snapshots with Dolby hard music in background. Silver screen illuminated with rays coming from a distant showed various emotions of life. Nobody knew "one new life was under rejuvenation on the last seats of the Inox cinema".

With the desire to hold and grow Rahul sat there with dilemma in mind whether to touch her or not. Five months of love was never diluted with a drop of lusty chemical.

Heena was under same convulsion, she too wanted to touch and be lost in his embrace but she sighed and her emotions dried.

"At times desperation burst out to bring up a new morning".

With all the zeal and courage Rahul reached for her hand and realized the warmth of Love, he got to know the real feel of Love, "he realized it was still summer inside them".

A smile covered Heena's exquisite face, while Rahul enjoyed the new bonhomie. Slowly fingers started travelling on the arms of chair trying to reach the half puzzle of fingers in order to complete it. Every touch and entangle was like a new orgasm, currents ran down her spine while Rahul felt something in his heart (It was the moment of lust bathed in love).

With the closed eyes and closed ears they heard everything unsaid and saw everything picturesque.

The entanglement was like "a travel of time". From the day they met to the day they will die together, everything crossed their closed eyes and made them smile.

"Love is a Beautiful Dream and everything beautiful in dream is Love".

Time slips like sand from hand when in love. Three hours movie kissed its end as the boy kissed the girl, breaking the plethora of pleasure Rahul and Heena went through (Pure Love). With the empty tub of popcorn and cups of soft drinks left with ice cubes, both stood and left for "eating" (or more playing).

When in love nothing can be better than AM LOVING IT space for eating. Rahul settled with his chicken stuff while his angel being a chocolate lover went for chocolate shake with veggie snacker (Yeah, these days it's a new trait!!! "Girls Going Veggie"; Is Kareena Responsible?) A general advice for all the girls "Eat Flesh In Order To Be Fleshy and Sexy..."

Rahul started with his chicken nuggets, Heena staring him phantasmagorical said "animal eating innocents" (given Heena was a hardcore pet lover).

Rahul replied, "You are the next innocent in queue...;)"

Heena winked and said, "With or without..."??

Rahul under shock, "Am I Getting Lucky Today, to use the thing in my wallet."

Heena slapping him in a naughty way spoke, my idea of concern was Ketchup!!! "You gonna eat this cute innocent girl with or without ketchup"...

"Molten Chocolate will be better I guess" Rahul quipped with a crispness in his voice.

"Ohk! But I thought you never liked chocolate" Heena teasingly.

"Who cares for the cherry when the Cake is your Favorite", Rahul answered smartly.

Heena with frowned eyebrows, "Hmmm, that's the reason am with you Asshole".

"You and your words always woo and leave me astonished".

"I Love You Rahul, Like No One Else Does", Heena said.

Rahul almost emotional replied quickly with "love you too", and they hugged.

Heena jerked off his hand saying, "I Need to Pee".

Oops, Rahul smirked.

Heena stood arranged her pullover and left for the washroom, when suddenly, in a low voice, Rahul said "Am I supposed to be in there with you".

Heena, under a shock almost screamed "Rahul, have you lost it", sudden outburst of Heena sent Rahul under shock and turbulence; he came up with "Sorry, you know my addiction and fantasy towards those clumsy hottie incidents from Porn movies..."

Heena with a stern look "Pathetic, asshole".

Rahul kept fantasizing about Heena unbuttoning and removing her jeans.

While she came back with an epitome smile on her face.

They both decided to call the day off, in her sweet little accent, Heena asked Rahul to drop her at her apartment.

She returned to her flat happy and exotic and found a packet at her doorstep with a message encrypted beautifully on it. "Happy five months anniversary" she read it out loud in her mind.

"Rahul is amazingly cute", she whispered thinking about him. Inside her flat, removing her pullover, she sat on her bed in her own languor with the received parcel. With ease and care she unveiled the things in packet and found some photographs with a letter, photos were new to her but Rahul was common in all of them, holding and kissing a hot girl dressed barely in her initials.

Heena, keeping herself calm kept the photos at side and started reading the letter.

"Hey, beautiful lots of hugs to you on your fifth anniversary with my Rahul (did I just write "My" that's because he is still mine). Heena, you are pretty, smart and Rahul is just an ordinary guy. So, it was very obvious "he falling for you".

Although you guys are together and closer from last five months, I and Rahul were never away, we were just separate.

Rahul missed me every day; he was always there to comfort me in sadness and in bed.

Rahul never lied to you about his love, maybe he is in love with you but he always kept me and our story much interesting, passionate and much hotter than yours.

Baby, you must be feeling weird about me and my letter, but baby, you know I pity on you when I see you roam around with the boy I owned and played with once.

P.S: photographs attached are my memoirs, citations for Rahul (u must be knowing he is awesome) and now mere evidence of our love."

Heena sat on her bed dumbstruck; her jolly mood got replaced with sadness and tears in eyes. Suddenly all love and promises seemed fatal to her. A beautiful life with Rahul which was doomed now seemed as bluff and lie. She started crying slowly and soon she was screaming in pain and distress; she felt cheated and lied.

All promises and good moments spent with Rahul crossed her eyes like a slide show with its end saying "It was all lie".

For once she thought of calling Rahul and beating the shit out of him but she settled with a short message service:

> Rahul my baby,
> It was great being with you (Last five months)
> All promises you made to me
> Made me feel like an angel
> But I never knew that "I was just another bitch and
> you were the dog behind".
> It's all over now;
> Your game, your lie and your Love.
> Hope to see you happy with your sexy Ankita.

Rahul, was lost in his dreams when his blackberry received a sms.

Enjoying his dreams Rahul hardly knew that his life was about to experience a night mare.

He woke up early, he had a headache; he checked his phone to see what the time is, he saw messages from Heena, he felt sorry for not being able to reply.

He read the messages intricately and his world came down all shattered over the floor. He was not sure of what he was reading and the mention of Ankita made him sweat profusely.

He called Heena up, she discarded his call, she was in no mood to talk, she hated him like never before; she felt cheated and disgusted.

Rahul wrote many messages to her, saying sorry and trying to explain, "it's a trap, and he is no more in touch with Ankita, last they met was before he started dating her".

Heena was adamant; she was neither answering his call nor replying to his sorry messages.

Out of blue, for once Heena received his call and thrashed him like anything,

"You freaking moron, don't ever call me up again; otherwise I will get you beaten up, I will make sure your each and every bone gets broken, freaking liar, cheat never ever call me up again".

Rahul went numb, he was unsure, his heart went through annihilation, and he lost his senses and was not speaking anything.

He stopped calling her.

Days turned sad and gloomy, he used to wait for her calls and messages, but she never called or texted him.

She blocked him on Facebook (Same place, where they met), changed her number and made sure none of her friend is in touch with Rahul.

Meanwhile, Rahul got busy with his writing career. One auspicious day, he came to know about the "Short Story writing competition" at his University.

He contacted the coordinator; the coordinator detailed him, "A national bestseller Author, has come up with an opportunity for students of LPU to be a National fame". He elaborated, "Fifteen best stories will be published in an Anthology and the best story of all will win a cash prize of INR. 30,000."

Rahul, made his mind, he knew it was his opportunity to be famous and the only way through which he can get Heena back into his life.

He disconnected himself from all diversions, no internet, no games, no parties, no hanging out with friends; only he and his story—the exquisite story of Rahul and Heena.

He started reading every Letter he wrote to Heena, when she was with him and when she is not with him. He read all the poems, he once dedicated to her.

He lived his love life once again; it was like a new birth with her. All those cute moments with her revisited his mind, he smiled thinking about them and very next moment became sad, realizing she is no more with him. He missed her in his life.

Heena-

She was missing him too, at times she wanted to go and hug him and let all the misunderstandings go away, but she couldn't do that, as she was a girl with principles and values, to forgive him was merely impossible for her, but he still had a chance to earn the apology from her.

Rahul wrote his story meticulously, he described every incident intricately and Heena's beauty passionately. He submitted the entry.

#Day of Result-

"I am alone this night and I'll tell you how it feels to be alone when you have experienced the clamorous following of the world. I'll tell you how it feels to be on the square one when you have known and scaled the heights. In this night of darkness, I'll tell how it feels to be alone in a bed when you have spent your nights in the arms of someone beautiful.

The stars outside my window and the ceiling inside, are more disappointed than I am, they miss you more than I do, they have seen me being the happiest person on the earth and when you return back, they will tell you how lonely I have been without you.

The ceiling is as cold as nascent oxygen. The emotions are as low as Indian economy and the depression is rushing higher to give Dollar a run for its status.

I have been on the other side of the night, when it was all rosy and coy and I am here too on the other side of bed, but there's a void, deep enough to succumb my whole life, there's an inescapable gap and there's a wearing feel of love.

I have been wrapped and cuddled, I have been kissed and teased and I have been pampered and spoiled. But all I remember is that I have been loved and ditched to mourn over it. You had made it easier for me and for my body to leap forward and make a dent in this world. But then I remember you going away, leaving me alone enough to flit between cry and 'don't cry'. I miss you more than I can say, I miss you more than I can feel and I miss you more than you can hear.

If there's one thing on this planet, I want right here right now, is—You…"

This was one prose he wrote for Heena; it was just that this time, he read it from his book, while Heena sat there in audience with wet eyes.

-x-x-x-

Back in car he kissed her and coaxed her to come for dinner with him. On the dinner table under the dim light of fluorescent bulb with soft sound of piano in background, he whispered to her, you have two options-

-Let me take you home and show you how much I missed you

Or

-Take me to your place and show me how much you missed me; with a radiant smile on her beautiful visage she said "don't make me crave for you".

Getting impatient, he uttered "my thirst is deeper".

"So, it's your time to hurt me, come", saying this she walked away towards the car, he got his signal and followed her. They drove to her place, climbing the stairs faster they reached her floor. Entering the apartment she asked "What do you want?" in the most seductive way.

"If you have anything remotely related with pain, give it to me" she hugged him so tight that he felt her heart beats on his chest.

Digging her face in his chest she kissed him on his mole, and like the sweat goes down, his hands were travelling on her beautiful body, slowly. She stood on her toes to reach his face and surrounding his cheek with both her hands she tried to kiss him, while his fingers made friendship with her soft and sensuous back.

Breaking the kiss dastardly she screamed "Go close the doors first."

With the irrepressible blazing speed he closed the door and whispered to her "Done! Now Love Me".

With her hands rushing through his hair and breathe getting heavier she squeezed him tight; her every touch made him impatient.

"In Love Only Distance Hurts, Come closer" he said holding up his world with her waist while his lips were playing tongue twister with hers... Breaking the kiss softly this time, she started unbuttoning him, with her squeeze his blood flow shot up, doing the honor he moved her gown a bit and kissed on her mole.

Taking his lips closer to her ear, he whispered the most genuine feeling he carried for her "You are the best thing happened to me and my life" and started eating her like an animal.

She trembled in pleasure and removed his shirt. Holding him close to her, she wrapped her long legs around his waist and said "Take Me in Your arms and Never Let Me Go". With the quickest movement of his finger her gown went down and the only separation between his tough and her soft body were initials. He kissed on her neck (he was waiting for it, since day one).

Kissing all over, circling the navel, he cupped her breasts softly, softer than softness.

Turning around she gave him a clear glimpse of her beautiful back with the perfect curves, with the one click the so called initials went off, with his fingers he freed her body from it and now her fluffy soft breast hung with freedom.

Hugging her tight he went for her softest part and kissed the left one (given the left hander he was); while his hands took the utmost care of her right, clutching him she tugged his head deep in her blossom. Holding her curves, he squeezed them. Going down he kissed on her beautiful legs, she felt a lightning in herself and a beautiful tear escaped her eyes.

He took her in his arms and kissed passionately involving most of the tongue and bites. She lied there beautiful and he stood there nervous, holding her by her waist he entered himself softly into her, she moaned and screamed his name in the most arousing manner and at last she buried herself in his arms. Kissing her, he found tears in her enormous beautiful eyes.

Love is more about trying to keep what you love even after knowing that it is going to change you forever.

Nazish Kondakari

A second year B.M.S student of Vidyalankar School of Information and Technology, Nazish is a 19 year old girl residing in Mumbai. She is an aspiring writer, author and an avid reader, with a huge collection of books. She loves pencil shading drawing (sketching) and painting.

Nazish has a blog by the name <u>kondkarinazish.wordpress.com</u>. She has also contributed articles to Novelist e-magazine and short story for an anthology by Sanmati Publishers. She has also interned as a content writer for at ADaring and Youthopia magazine.

You can reach her at - <u>Kondkarinazish95@gmail.com</u>

3

CHILDHOOD MEMORIES OF UNNAMED FEELINGS WITH A PINCH OF FRIENDSHIP!

Nazish Kondkari

It is a Sunday morning, and I am reading newspaper with my Sunday refreshing cup of coffee. My daughter, Mira; age 16 is a big bookworm. She comes with her novel, and is sitting confused on the couch. I have never seen her, this silent and lost ever. She is very talkative sweet and innocent, and the only one after my wife that makes me feel good even if I am tired after heavy loads of work.

My wife, Nisha is in the kitchen and busy with her chores while my younger son is busy playing his games. "Mira," I called out, "what is that's bothering you princess?" I asked her worriedly, she looks at me in a sudden shocked expression and asks me "Dad, how do you know that I am thinking something?" "Well, it's you who always say that your dad is your best friend and now you hiding something from your best friend?" I said. "Nah, dad I am not hiding. I am just upset with this novel story. It was an incomplete love story of a guy's first love. And it is such a despondent and heart wrenching story. Why people meet if they are not meant to be?

Her question took me to my past. Something that I had forgotten about and today, my daughter's innocent question and the melancholy feeling on her face took me to an inexplicable feeling of my past. It was time to make my daughter understand the ups and downs of life and how to deal with them. And so I decided to share with her a story.

I took her gentle soft hand and told her to come with me. We went towards the balcony and sat on the chairs with an awed nature and breeze encompassing us. I looked at her and she felt calm in that scenario out in the open breeze "Princess I have always guided you to the right path, and no matter whatever happens I and your mom are always with you whenever you need us. Now that you are grown up; you will face the new world out there very soon. You will meet new people and some feelings would surround you that will be new to you. But sometimes it happens that people come in your life to teach you something, to make you realize that you are strong and can fight back the situations that might make you weak. And so your dad has something to share with you, that might help you understand how life plays well and you need to learn to tackle the situation bravely."

She was listening in an inquisitive manner. "This is virginal to my childhood and my first crush or may be love." "Really dad? Your first love??? Tell me tell me about it please.." she jumped on her chair with euphoria. "Easy princess". I used to live with your dada dadi in a small society. I was 6 years old. I used to do lot of mischief. I had friends of my age with whom I used to play cricket, football, and slowly we had also formed a group of friends which included girls as well. Raj uncle who comes to meet us every vacation from Delhi is my friend since those days. We were both partners in mischief and crimes around. We even used to go school together and study together.

One day, there was a new comer who shifted in our society and with them something new entered in my life. We all were playing when this car came and stood in our compound which halted our game and then we had to wait till the car moved. A sweet little chubby bubbly girl, just like you got out from the car. She was innocent and adorable; her brown eyes and lovely straight hair with those dimples on her cheeks. She got down from the car, while her mom got busy with their luggage. She was looking at the buildings, with her bag pack on her shoulders and a lovely doll in her hand. She was of my age. She saw us and gave a lovely smile. She came towards us while we all were looking at her beauty as she had all the sparkling feeling around her and we were just stunned looking at her. "Hie, I am Pari, do you all stay here?" We all nodded our heads in affirmation. "Oh! So that's great, can I join you all to play from tomorrow. I am very new in this society and city. I stay at err…. Wait I'll ask my mom and come." Her cute confused gesture made me feel like pinching her cheeks. She ran to her mom, and asked her something and came back running to us. While panting she said, "I stay at 6th floor A wing. Will you all mind if I come to play with you all?"

All others looked at each other thinking what answer should we give, but I took a step ahead and answered. "Sure, Pari, you can join us anytime you want. We will be happy to welcome a new friend in our group, right friends?" Everyone nodded to give positive answer.

"Pari, let's go home, what you doing there?"

Yes mom! See I made new friends." she shouted back to answer her mother.

Her mother came towards us and was delighted to meet us as well as to see how her sweet daughter made friends in such less time. Her mother, Miss. Khanna introduced herself as well as asked each one our names. When she asked me I flamboyantly replied, Arjun Malhotra. And she pinched my cheeks and told Pari, to come back to her friends tomorrow as they had loads to arrange in their new home.

"Can we all help you?" Raj asked aunty.

Hearing this aunty smiled and said, "You kids are very helpful and good mannered I am happy that my daughter has made good friends here. But no kids, the things are heavy to carry and are dangerous for you all."

"Okay aunty." We all agreed. Pari and aunty waved us bye. And they went to their home.

"Where is Pari's dad? He was not there with them?" Raj asked,

To this Deepti opened her mouth; Deepti was kind of straight forward and gossip kind of a girl just like her mother. Deepti was our society's secretary's daughter. "Oh! She is the lady, my mom dad were talking about her yesterday. Dad was telling mom that there is a new lady coming to stay in our society with her little daughter. The lady is divorcee."

"Divorcee! What does that mean?" I asked.

"Oh you dumb! You don't know what is divorce? Divorce is when your parents decide to stay separate and live their life without each other. They are no more called husband-wife."

We went to our respective home and I was still wondering what Deepti told us. That night I did not have dinner; your dadi thought I am purposely not having my dinner; I just at one chapatti to get away from her scolding. But then she saw me silent the next morning, missed my play too, she came and asked me what was wrong with me. It was then I cried hugging her and told her, "Ma, please don't be a divorcee, tell dad not to leave us alone. I'll listen to you both and never trouble you both". She was shocked to hear what I had said and asked me who told me about the divorce thing? I narrated the previous day's incidence and what Deepti told us. Then she smiled, and told me, that it is not necessary that every married couple gets separated. There are times when things don't work and the couples decide to separate. She kissed my forehead and told me, that your dad won't leave us and go. He loves us a lot and that they will never get divorced. But she also asked me for a promise that I will not speak or discuss about divorce in front of Pari or her mother. They will feel bad. And so I promised her that I won't talk about it in front of them.

Then I ran down to play with my bat, and then I saw Pari and others already down playing badminton.

"Hey hi!" she greeted me.

"Hi." I greeted her back, y

"You are with your bat? You want to play cricket?" Pari asked me.

"Yes," Deepti interrupted, "Krish loves to play cricket. So now all boys will play cricket and we girl's badminton."

"Noooo!!..." I said, "I mean we all boys and girls will together play badminton. Cricket we can play later."

Days passed by, we all used to play badminton, hide and seek and many more games together. It was fun to play with Pari. Her innocence used to make us laugh. And I also took care that no one would ask Pari about her dad. Her mom used to sometimes treat us with chocolates. Her mom used to go office and come back in evening, and on Sundays she used to play with us all. Her mom and my mom also became good friends. This got me closer to Pari. Pari was admitted to my school itself. I Raj and Pari became good friends as we shared the same school. Our homework, studies and play was never done without each other. Sometimes Pari used to have lunch at my place as her mom used to be busy. My mom dad treated Pari well, just like their own daughter.

Seeing this Deepti became jealous as she did not like Pari being my and Raj's close friend. She always searched for something or the other, to make Pari feel bad. One day I and Raj were just sitting down in our building discussing about the cartoons and movies, Pari had gone with her mom for shopping. When she came back, Deepti took the advantage and greeted aunty and Pari. Aunty went ahead as she was on a call and Pari and Deepti were talking. Raj saw Pari crying and running towards her home. Deepti had a wicked smile on her face. Raj made me see Pari, crying towards her building.

I and Raj went towards Deepti to ask, why Pari was crying. Deepti told us, she was missing her dad and was upset. I and Raj rushed towards her home to make her feel nice.

The door was slightly open when we heard Pari talking to her mom. "Princess, why are you crying sweetie?"

"Mom, that Deepti, I don't like her, she always make me realize that I don't have my dad, and keeps talking about her father in front of me and upset me. Mom why does she do this to me? I never did anything bad to her."

Her mom hugged her and saw me and Raj at the door. I and Raj gestured aunty not to let Pari know that we were there and we quietly escaped and I rushed down in anger towards Deepti. Raj followed me as he knew I will be flowing like lava on Deepti now. I ran towards Deepti she was down with other friends bragging about her gifts and clothes she got new from her uncle.

"Deepti…" I shouted so loud that everyone was shocked and scared to see me red in anger and panting heavily. Raj was making me calm and telling me to sit and talk properly. But I did not listen to him.

"What happened Krish why are you so angry?" Deepti asked.

"You fool, stupid, monkey, donkey, how could you make Pari cry? I had warned you not to talk about her dad in front of her why do you have to do all this? Enough is enough Deepti; I always ignored your foolishness and stupidity till now. But not anymore, you both tell Pari and her mom, sorry and promise us all you won't do all this again or else I won't allow you to play with us. Listening this everyone agreed to me.

"Yes! Deepti you owe sorry to Pari". Raj replied. To this Deepti responded in a rude way, "Why should I say sorry? And why are you all against me all of a sudden? Why does she always get all the attention she wants and not me?"

"Ask that to yourself, Deepti. Choice is yours now. Do you want us all not to talk to you or you're apologizing to Pari and her mom."

"Krish you can't do this to me? You are my best buddy."

"If I am your best buddy then prove it. Go and say sorry to them." I said a bit louder which shook Deepti and all others. No one had seen me this angry ever. Everyone thought I was calm. But seeing tears in Pari's eyes made me mad and Deepti behavior was adding on to it.

Finally Deepti trailed towards Pari's house and we followed her. She jumped and rang the doorbell with her head down; Pari's mom opened the door and greeted us all with a sad smile. We saw Pari sad, and upset sitting on her swing in her small balcony with her teddy tightly hugged. Deepti stepped inside the house and went towards Pari. We all followed Deepti and stood away with Pari's mom.

Pari saw us and Deepti. "I am sorry Pari, I am extremely sorry to hurt you and make you cry and I promise I won't talk to you about your dad again" Deepti turned towards aunty, "Aunty I am sorry to you too." Pari smiled and said "It's okay Deepti" and she hugged Deepti as well." "My mom says if you hug someone they feel nice." Aunty smiled. And so we all did. After that day, Deepti, never tried to hurt Pari, in fact they became good friends and started sharing girls talk with each other.

We were in 6th grade, that time and days later; I and Raj realized Pari's birthday was around the corner. I was super excited. I had specially bought a small note pad, and started writing things what all I need and what all I will do for her birthday. It was like I became a planner. I used to carry my small notepad everywhere in my pocket. As the ideas used to come in, I used to write down in my small notepad diary. One day, Raj came to my home and I showed him my planning.

We were in the bedroom and I was on and on with the arrangements and planning details. "Krish, do you like Pari?" Raj asked me.

"Oh! Yes of course, she is so sweet and innocent just like fairies described in fairy tales", I replied busy playing with the ball throwing towards the wall and catching.

"No! Krish I meant, do you like her as a girlfriend or you have a crush on her?" I missed the catch and I looked towards Raj in shocked as if someone caught me copying during exams or having ice cream secretly.

"Shushhhh! Are you mad, mom will listen!" I answered him.

"That means you really like her?" Raj asked smiling wickedly.

"No, I mean, I don't know what you are asking about." I said in confused manner not looking towards him.

"You idiot, you are trying to hide from me huh! It's clearly written on your face. Yahoooooo, Krish has feelings for Pari."

I pulled him in shock smiling sheepishly and put my hand on his mouth to shut him. Thank god mom did not hear him that time as she was busy with her work in the hall.

We had told mom, to order cake, and asked aunty not to wish Pari on her birthday and act as if she forgot. Aunty was happy to see us planning for Pari to make her feel special. And all the arrangements were done. Deepti had to bring Pari to my place as I had decided to surprise her. I, mom and my friends had decorated my house. I had also got a silver crown for her. Aunty had got nice gown for her. Everything was perfectly done. I, Raj and Deepti had prepared a funny dance for Pari. We all were waiting for Pari to come. Deepti had told Pari, that I have got fever so that she would come rushing to my home to see me. The plan was executed. It all happened the way we thought. Pari came rushing towards my home. She pushed the door which was kept open it was all dark, as she came in calling my name and my mom's name. As she came in the middle scared, the lights were lit on and we all shouted in delight surprising her with party hats on our head, we all shouted in echo HAPPY BIRTHDAY PARI. I was on my knees in front of her, and the balloon filled with sparkles was burst and the fan was turned on which had petals of flowers which came down on her. And she was so surprised and that smile on her face was one in a million smiles for me.

Her mom hugged her and kissed her and she was so delighted looking at the arrangements. She said "I thought you all forgot my birthday". "How can we forget your birthday, but this all was planned by Krish. Her mom told to her. She looked at me with sparkling eyes and a beautiful smile. Her mom took her inside and dressed her. As she came outside, I was stunned looking at her beauty. She was looking like a perfect beauty in that white gown of hers just like a Barbie, or Cinderella or some another beauty princess. My mom too kissed her, and complimented her she is looking adorable. She ran towards me and asked me "Krish how am I looking?" "ummmm… something is missing, don't you think Raj? Um.. Yeah Krish I too think something is missing. Her smile was slowly fading, when I took the crown that I was hiding in between the gift boxes and put on her head immediately. She looked surprised with her eyes wide open. "Now it's perfect, just like a real princess." I said smiling. She hugged me tight and everyone looked at us. I saw mom and aunty smiling I think even they had sensed that I and Pari shared a different feeling more than friendship.

We did cake cutting ceremony and enjoyed the party. As everyone finished eating the snacks, I Raj and Deepti rushed to wear our costumes. My mom helped us all three in getting dressed. We went out in our funny costumes and played a small skit which was followed by dance. I could see how Pari was laughing and enjoying the program. Later she too joined us dancing and then everyone joined. We all enjoyed the dance, food, talks and games. Pari was happy to see so many gifts. My dad had gone out for some office work that day, but he did not forget to wish Pari, with a phone call. She was happier to receive my dad's call. All were tired and were heading towards home. Mom had convinced aunty to stay at our place as even my dad was not there.

I had made a special card for Pari which I gave her, when mom and aunty were busy in their talks, and cleaning the house. She had tears in her eyes. I was shocked to see those tears and I wiped them asking her what was wrong, to which she giggled and told, "You stupid, these are tears of happiness. You made me feel so special. You are a special friend and very close to my heart. Thanks Krish, for everything you have done for me." And we hugged.

From that day, I and Pari shared a special feeling. Our studies were done together. I tried my level best to make sure Pari never cried. She was everything to me. Though we never told each other about our feelings but it was understood by both of us. I also remember that sometimes I and Pari used to climb our society's tamarind tree and sit on thee brance for hours having tamarinds, talking stuff, cracking jokes, sharing secrets and once Pari even kissed me on my cheeks and I was smiled feeling shy.

One Sunday morning, Pari came panting, scared and was crying as she came to our home. We were having breakfast. She had fear in her eyes when mom opened the door; I saw her crying. I rushed towards her. "Aunty, uncle, my mom is not responding, she is not answering to me. She is deeply asleep. I don't know she never did this. I told her I am hungry, but she is not uttering a word, I think she went unconscious, she was not well since many days, I saw her weak and falling on the floor at times. Please come with me she cried harder." My mom dad got scared and rushed towards Pari's home I was told to take care of Pari. Dad on the way called Raj and Deepti's parents and the doctor too.

Pari was crying but she had held my hand tightly and was not ready to leave. She was continuously crying and seeing her even I started crying.

"Shush!! Pari, please stop crying."

My mom will be alright na Krish?"

"Yes she will be."

And I hugged her back to make her feel good. After sometime, me, Pari, Raj and Deepti went to Pari's home to see what was happening. When we reached there, I saw my mom crying, my dad deeply upset, while Pari's mom was laid down on white cloth. Pari saw her mom in the white cloth and was broken to see that her mom had left her alone@ We all were broken and were in shock to see aunty dead. Pari, fell on her knees and started crying. I held her in my arms and she kept crying keeping her head on my chest. I, Raj and Deepti cried hugging her. My mom checked aunt's cell phone and called someone. Pari was holding her mom's dead hand in her hands crying and asking why did you leave me alone mom. I sat beside Pari, holding her other hand.

In some time, an old lady in white dress entered the room with tears in her eyes. "Pari…" she called out,

"Grandma…"

Pari cried loud and ran towards her. They hugged each other.

"Grandma… What happened to mom, why did she leave me alone? She had promised me she will never leave me like dad left me." Pari cried hard, and seeing her in pain even I started crying. It was time to take the dead body for the funeral ritual. While taking the dead body, Pari ran behind the body stopping everyone"

"Please don't take away my mom, come back mom" she shouted.

My mom was taking care of her grandma and I ran behind Pari to stop her. She falls in my arms and cried hard. "Krish stop them, they are taking my mom away, please stop them. I hugged her tight crying. My mom told me, that night that Pari's mom had disease known as cancer, which she hid from us all and Pari, so that the few days she had left, she would spend happily with Pari and not upset her.

After some days' my mom gave me a shock that Pari will be leaving with her grandma the next day. I was thunderstruck by those words.

"No mom, I cried hard and louder "please tell her grandma not to take her away I will take care of her, we will take care of her."

My mom hugged me to calm me down and made me understood, that Pari is in depression. She needs to be taken away from this place and people who will remind her of her mom. She had seen her mom's dead body.

"Son! Let her go, it will be best for her as if she will stay here, this place and people will always remind her of her mom's and memories related to her mother. Don't you want to see her happy and like she was before?"

I understood her condition and what mom was trying to say. I agreed with mom. With a heavy heart, I prepared some gifts and card which contained a note written by me:

Pari; please always keep smiling and be happy in your life, I wish you good luck for your future. When you leave this place and go to a new place leave all your pains and sorrows here and live a new life. Please be happy and keep smiling. Yours lovingly Krish.

I gave her an album of all our group photos in it. Her and my photos, her birthday's photos, some cards made by me and gifts. I promised myself to smile in front of her and make her feel good for the last time and wave her goodbye. The day when she was leaving; we all came down to wave her goodbye and give her flowers and gifts. I had told everyone not to cry in front of her. We all gave her gifts, smiled made her smile and laugh and hugged her. My mom dad hugged and kissed her and told that they would miss their daughter a lot. She met me; we exchanged smiles which we knew was full of pains. She hugged me tightly and I hugged her back. I kissed her forehead handing her, her gifts and cards. She went towards the car, faked a smile waved us bye gave me a flying kiss. Sat in the car and the car drove away. I, Raj and Deepti stood there watching the car go. Till the car vanished I smiled and then tears rolled down in my eyes. I was broken but both my hands were held tightly by Deepti and Raj. My mom too had tears in her eyes.

She had left a letter for me in my pocket while hugging. I realized at night while changing. I opened it furiously. She had written the same memories that we shared and wished me luck and happiness. She had also written that she will miss me a lot. And down there it was written that her real name was not Pari... After some pause ...

What was her real name dad? My daughter asked curiously. "I smiled and replied it was Mira."

Ayushi Nayan

Ayushi Nayan, born in Jharkhand, had a flair for writing ever since she was a child. She is a nature-lover too and likes designing things in her own way. She is currently residing in Kolkata and pursuing B.Sc in Textile Designing.

You can reach her at - ayushinayan05@gmail.com

4

KARMA INSTANTLY SLAPPED HER BACK

Ayushi Nayan

"*I wanna be a trustworthy daughter-I wanna be a victorious son.*

I wanna be an adorable sister & a freakish brother.

I wanna be an enchanting stranger-I wanna be a beautiful known personality.

I wanna be an allegiant husband & a chaste, idealized wife.

I wanna be the one-in-a million sort of father & an endearing, sacrificing mother.

I wanna be a loved past-I wanna be a tantalising, craved future."

****

"Reminiscence isn't just your memory alone. Sometimes, it has several other memories entwined with them, thus making it hard to bury!"

It was a Sunday & I was enjoying my holiday, beautifully. Deeply indulged in one of the best books "What Happens Next" by the most loved author, Kirtan Shivroy. The automated machine-voice of the clock in the Coffee Day Club spoke, "The time is 10:30 A.M.", I looked outside, and it was raining heavily.

"I won't give up... Even this way gets rough..." one of the most soothing songs was being played at the CDC.

"A Sunday, a lovely book, a soothing song, rain and a cup of coffee. A perfect bliss, yeah?" I whispered to myself.

Suddenly came an adorable girl gushing inside, wearing pajama and a black hoodie on top of a pink top, all soaked in water.

'*Beautiful!*' I whispered. She scanned the whole club, there wasn't a single chair empty, but the only one beside me. She hastily sat on it, adjusted herself and kept a diary properly wrapped in transparent poly-bag on the table.

'Oh-My-God!' the words just slipped out of my mouth, on seeing her badly burnt left hand. Thankfully she didn't hear me-or she must have ignored. I wondered how it happened. She placed her white leather bag on her lap, and ordered a cup of black coffee. From her bag, she took out a book 'Destruction of the Beasts', by Arita Singh and started studying it. Yeah! I had been noticing her each and every move-why shouldn't I? She was heavenly pretty.

After an hour, she hung her bag, and moved towards the billing counter. I desired to talk to her, but I had been totally engaged in starring at her. I watched her pay the bill, and then she exited. I wished she'd once look at me, but who was I to her-a stranger-perfectly unknown.

I returned to my book, again losing myself in the perfect ecstasy. Minutes later, I looked at my watch and my eyes fell on the diary which she left on the table.

'Fifteen minutes have passed and I don't think I would find her, but this may be... important', I spoke to myself taking out the diary from the poly-bag hoping I could find some contact details about her. I leafed through the first few pages, it was empty. Diaries are mainly used to pen down one's innermost feelings, so I flipped through the pages to look at what it contained.

An inner page read:

"TELLING PEOPLE A FICTION IS PAINLESS. BUT PENNING DOWN ONE'S MEMORIES AND GETTING THEM PUBLISHED AS A NON-FICTION IS LIKE SCRATCHING ONE'S OWN FLESH IN FRONT OF A LION AND HOPING IT WOULD JUST PASS BY, WITHOUT WOUNDING YOU!"

The word '*Publish*' knocked my mind. I being a publisher was always in search of stories that would send a shiver down the readers' bodies. I knew something marvelous was lying inside it, so I got ready for the sentimental journey.

The next page read: **"The Darkest Days of My Life"**:

We were lying on the bed, our bodies covered with the sheet, but our soul was naked in front of each other. She was ruffling my hair, whispering I Love You in broken syllables. I'd my head placed on her chest and tears from my eyes touched her bare chest.

"Never leave me. Without you, I can't even wonder about my existence." I sobbed. She swiftly wiped away my tears bringing my face close to hers.

"You know what? I am the mere world, but you are its components. A world can exist without them, but it serves no purpose, thus it withers within days. Even if we get straggled someday, I'd vanish; I'd vaporize as being left with no life. You're my life, how can I leave you?" she whispered onto my lips. Her voice, velvet soft.

She wasn't a literate, but she had magic in her words, and no person would suppose her to be less than an educated.

We were searching for a hope in each other's eyes, a hope of togetherness. She took me in her arms, and sniffed my hair.

Suddenly the door was pushed hard leaving it open, making us the spectacle. They were here-our parents. On seeing them, we were horror-struck, even able to hear each other's heartbeat not because of the closeness, but because of the fear. Our body trembled with horror-for this was going to be the end of our love story or may be 'us'. We went scarlet, aware of their presence. Our mothers glared at us, as our fathers left with a disgust on their faces, muttering something under their breath.

We were left alone for a minute, to get dressed, tears continuously streaming down from our eyes. The last thing we did before leaving the room was to hug each other & our eyes made an impossible promise - everything would soon be fine.

My parents didn't speak to me until her family left. They being educated, knew how to handle a situation. But I knew from her parents' face what she'd have to go through.

I got a knockout scolding and all medium of communication was snatched away, besides I was grounded for two months, which meant I couldn't even see her.

A week later:

I woke up and just as I was about to enter the hall, I heard my parents mentioning her name 'Karuna'. I overheard the conversation that followed.

"Where's she, now?" my mom inquired with a touch of anger in her voice.

"Staying with her cousins", my dad said.

"Has she recovered from it?"

"Yes. She's perfectly fine, smiling, laughing and playing around with her cousins. Just the scars on the skin are too deep to heal so early."

My mom sighed. "Kids these days. They call this love. Weird!"

"Forget it. Rishika's recovering now. Also Karuna is going to get engaged to a boy, Vikash. By the way, I am thankful to us that we arrested our anger in control, otherwise…"

"Karuna's getting married? This would be painful news for Rishika. And yeah, by when are we supposed to leave?"

"Within a week. Not more than that. Start packing."

What? Where were we leaving for? And why? What about Karuna? She is happy! The girl who was promising me a few days ago that she would die without me, is now happy? Playing around… Smiling? How can that smile rest on her face, without me? I sobbed.

Suddenly, I heard foot-steps approaching me, so I ran to my room. I locked the door behind me, and sat on the floor, my head between my knees, I wanted to scream, but it got choked somewhere in my throat. I wanted to burst in a cry, but all I did was nothing.

Everything came crashing down at my feet. I failed to engulf the fact that she's happy without me! The girl for whom I'd been constantly crying, to meet her, to see her, was happy in her own world! All promises broken, the love vanished somewhere or maybe she never loved me. Did she find someone else, better than me? Or has she fallen for a guy? Uncountable thoughts were encompassing me. Anger enveloped me, and I didn't know how come I developed infuriation for her, for my love.

'If not mine, then no one else's too', I grimaced. I made a plan to destroy her. I waited for the night, when my parents' would sleep. I secretly went into their room, the lock being luckily opened; I took my mother's cellphone and ran back to my room. I called one of my trusted neighbours, Rakesh. I asked him to bring a bottle of sulphuric-acid that could burn anything, anything! Yes, I planned to disfigure her face, so that no one would ever love her; the worst mistake of my life. He questioned me nothing as he trusted me, and knew I would do no ill; he was wrong for the very first time. He promised me that I'd get it by 11 in the morning, the next day.

It's a truth that when a person is trapped in bad phases, for him, his anger, his pain, his wrong ways seems to bring justice. And I was going through the same phase.

After disconnecting the call, I deleted his number from the call list, and kept the cellphone in mom's room. I went to my bed, but I couldn't sleep that night. I was tossing over my bed with pain & rage. My tears were soaked by the pillow on which once she laid her head.

I got ready by 10:45 a.m. the next day. I even covered my face, leaving just my eyes exposed. I went to the hall, it was empty, it came to my notice that my Dad had left for his work and my mom must be sleeping.

I stepped out of my house, in the way I found Rakesh. He furtively handed over the bottle to me. I paid him, and hurried over to her cousin's house. Yes! I knew, not just this place but every place of her relative, she'd told me when we 'were' together. Hostility and revenge now engulfed me.

I reached her cousin's place within seven minutes. I hid behind the tree, waiting impatiently for her arrival. My hands did not even tremble once. Jeez. How cruel I had been! Ten minutes had passed still there was no sign of her. As I took a step towards her cousin's house, I saw her coming, her hands were scarred and yes they were too deep, as my father said. Appeared as if someone burnt her hand with a rod-must be her father. She had a smile on her face, I didn't care if it was a real or a fake one, I just wanted that smile to disappear forever.

I cautiously broke the seal of the bottle and with long steps I followed her. As she turned back I spilled the acid over her beautiful, angelic face. She shrieked with pain, lay there squirming, shouting 'Acid! Acid!', & I fled away. I wanted to tell her 'This is how I felt when I heard that you were happy without me.'

While I was on the way home, I stumbled over a rock and the little amount of acid that was still there in the bottle, splashed on my left hand. It was a very, very bad sensation, my skin felt like the thawing plastic when heated with fire. I stifled my immense pain & my shriek within myself. I found a small pond near-by and dipped my hand in the water. I soon regretted for what I did. Being a strong girl, I pulled out a hankerchief tugged in my pajama, soaked it in water and tied it on my hand.

Karma isn't a bitch, it's like a rubber-hand. If you try to stretch a rubber-hand more than what it can handle, it slaps you back-and that's exactly what Karma does!

I was punished for my deed instantly. *"WHEN ONE DOES ILL, KARMA DOESN'T SLAPS ALONE, ONE'S ACTIONS DOES TOO."* I realized how wrong I was about my pain in front of hers, at times the acid-burning hurts more than love, even more than betrayal. Betrayal leaves an unseen scar on your soul, but Acid leaves a physical as well as a mental wound, not just a scar.

I still disguise myself for hating her for doing something no one deserves.

I was dying with pain. Within three minutes I got home, and told my mother whatever happened. Her face was expressionless but tears revealed her feelings. She called my dad, and I was taken to the City Hospital, about two kilometers from where we resided. The doctor there was my Dad's best friend, so all my surgeries were secretly carried out.

I was wondering about Karuna, what she must be going through. I rued, for doing that to her. This wasn't my peccadillo; this was one of the greatest sins people do to destroy others. I knew I won't be ever remitted.

After the surgery we moved to a new city, too far from the previous one. I resisted going, but they told me that I would be caught, and I didn't want to be.

I once again asked my dad about Karuna. Jeez! I can't describe the feeling that travels down from my brain to my feet when I utter her name. My dad stayed mum. I know I had affronted all of them.

I'd been talking to Rakesh, to know what's going on with Karuna. He liked me, I knew this from the very beginning, but I couldn't accept the fact being in love with her. After the occurrence of those incidents, I realized I could trust him forever.

By maintaining a contact with him, I'd been getting every details about Karuna. Although she was in distress, and knew I did this to her, she never cursed me.

With each passing day, grew my guilt. She had said '*The world would vanish without its components.* 'But what if the components harm the world?-*The components too would die within days.* Here am I after seven years of that incident full of regret but not yet tired of missing her, still flooded with guilt and the strength to ask for forgiveness.

I wanted to throw up all the guilt I've been holding inside me, and so I decided that the world should know about my evil deed. Although, I knew could be caught, yet I wanted to do this, I wanted to step on the stairs of justice, giving myself a chance to be forgiven-by getting this story published.

Back there what had happened was -

Hearing her scream, her neighbours came and took her to a local hospital. The doctors there worsened her case. I burnt her face and chest, the chest I laid my head on, some days before. When she was admitted she uttered my name. Her family thought it was me who did this. They were correct, but she told them she wanted to meet me, again an impossible thing, she asked for 'us.' She lost her hair, brows and eyelashes, she lost her beauty, and she gained pain-for doing nothing! My angel, my sinless cherub.

Her parents got loan, with the help of their relatives. They admitted her in the City-Hospital where once I had been. Her surgeries were done, but I had left scars on her face, wounds in her heart that would never go, never heal.

Exactly after one year, her parents forced her for marriage. From a list they told her about a guy who wasn't demanding dowry, but her, but she ignored. They knew she hadn't yet recovered, still they wanted her to step up on the stairs of difficulties and responsibilities.

Vikash, her fiance declined the marriage proposal at first, but later he asked for a solitary meeting. Their parents sent her to him, where Vikash tried to rape her. But luckily she fled from his grip. She didn't go home, but ran to a nearby village and sheltered herself in an old muddy house, for that night.

At a very young age, she had lost her love, who later on, burnt her face with acid. She wasn't even fully recovered when her fiancé tried to molest her. She was lacking the strength to continue her life. So finally she had decided to end her life, her purposeless life.

It was a bright morning but she wasn't, she got fresh and wore the same dress she had been wearing since yesterday. The people who had been throwing sympathetic looks on her, she asked them the directions to a medicine store. On following the directions, she reached there, keeping her face calm & paltering a fake smile. A boy approached her, half of his face was burnt, an acid burn; she recognized, who knew it better than her. She knew how it felt to get the 'Oh-I-Am-So-Sorry-For-You' looks, so she didn't gaze at him.

"Sleeping pills", she said boldly, to the chemist.

"I've lost my prescription. Can you give me an ointment to heal this burn-an acid burn", the boy said almost at the same moment the girl finished.

"Sorry to both of you, I can fulfil none of your needs as I am out stocks these days", the chemist lied. 'Both of them are suffering from the same thing, yet their perception is so different. One wants to die while the other wants to try', he thought.

Both of them sat on the bench lying under the Banyan tree. They looked at each other, lips pressed tight.

"So an acid burn?" she asked, few minutes later.

"Hmm... Yes", he answered starring at the ground.

"Who did it?"

The boy thought for a moment whether to tell her or not.

"I did this", he said with a saint smile & proudness on his face.

"But for what?" Her brows furrowed. All negativism gone, all suicidal thoughts vanished for a moment.

"I know. You're trying to save her, yeah? But we can't save them from the guilt they are drowning in, now."

"No, not at all! It would have been a privilege to get hurt by her. But she left me alone, and so I had to do this."

He discovered from her expressions that she didn't understand what he meant. Sure she did, but she was just bewildered.

"We both loved each other, she had brain tumour and she... Left me! Here, I am, all alone to die. She loved my soul much more than my face. I couldn't damage my soul anymore, it had already been damaged due to her absence. And so I decided to disfigure my face, not wanting to be desired by anyone else apart from her. I had no one else, but she. But now..." and he broke down.

She was struck by the greatness of his love, and awed by his loyalty. She could still be felt in his words, in him.

He cocked his head to one side, sighed deeply and asked, "What about you?"

She looked into the depth of his eyes, and saw the 'you-can-trust-me' look.

She slowly started and saw various sort of expressions, smile to anger, and pain to relief - hugging his face one after the other.

"Do you still miss her? And was she the one who did this to you?" he asked when she stopped, gesturing towards his hand. She noticed him wiping away the tears, while he cocked his head to one side.

"Yes to both the questions. I can understand her anger, her pain. I wish I could just talk to her once. I searched her all over our place but got to know nothing about where she resides."

"In guilt, probably" his eyes filled with fury.

Then they chatted for a while about their family and friends.

He stood, to leave. "You can stay with my aunt, she lives alone, beside she is a good person", he said with the 'You-can-trust-me' look once again.

Her face was filled with uncertainty.

"I would show you the place. I am sure you'd have no problem."

She nodded, relieved.

He took her to a house-she couldn't believe that this house could ever exist in any corner of that village. His aunt provided her the basic necessities, and she treated her like her own daughter.

Their company to each other was thirst quenching. The smile that was lost somewhere in the disastrous journey, returned hopping to them, happily. It looked like autumn just dropped by spring into their lives.

They freed themselves of their fear. It was acknowledged by both of them, that they had started liking each other, until one day, when his aunt asked them about marriage, they realized that the body needs the soul forever, and it wasn't just affection, it was love-the chaste love.

"I can't marry against my parents' wish and they are against love-marriage." she went scarlet as the last word slipped out of her mouth.

"My instincts say that they would agree. Aunt will also accompany us", he promised.

His aunt nodded, her promising eyes said everything will be okay.

She smiled, keeping all sorts of anticipations at a bay.

The next day they went to her town. The people there saw them, but not with sympathy, they smiled at them. She was now so habituated to those sympathetic looks that its absence was kind of weird to her.

They reached her home, where her father and mother were standing at the door-step.

'He would beat the hell out of me and would chuck me out of the house saying you don't deserve to be a daughter & my mom standing behind him, all cold, would nod. Then she would come up to me, and shut the door on my face', this is how she imagined the situation to be like.

But always happens the unexpected.

His father smiled & hugged her tightly. Her mother was watching them, unstoppable tears were running down from her eyes. Karuna was confused. She couldn't understand what was going on. 'I ran away from here, I'm returning after one year, what made them react in a calm way, what's the matter?' she wondered.

As her dad released her, her mother grabbed her. When her mom freed her from her motherly-grip, she noticed her dad touching Tarun's aunt's feet, then he hugged Tarun, as well. She gaped at them, totally puzzled.

Finally her Dad broke the silence.

"He is Tarun. You know him better than me, but I've been knowing him for years. His Aunt and me have been great friends", he said while leading them to the front room.

"When you fled away, we searched for you all over our small town, but no one had seen you. The next day when I was going to file your missing report in the police station, I got a call from Tarun." he said smiling at Tarun.

He grinned back.

"Tarun told me that you were with him, and everything that happened with you. We knew Tarun, and trusted him. Well, do you remember your father once mentioned about a guy, who demanded for a pure soul, no dowry, nothing! Here is that lovely boy!", suddenly her face was expressionless.

"Sorry sweety, we are the worst parents anyone could ever have. We left you alone, when you wanted to shed your tears and pain on our shoulders." and her mom broke down.

Now it was my turn to take her in arms, I hurried. Even Devils can't bear seeing mothers' tears, so how could an innocent girl with magnanimous heart could avoid her mother?

"Mom, look it is okay. Providentially we all are happy, nowhere was your fault. I had bad times written in my fate but now, it's over. If god's gifts you with pain, then for the incoming days, he has kept the doubled happiness of it, awaiting for us", as I wiped her tears, Tarun came, and hugged both of us. "Please don't cry, ladies", he said. She punched him on his chest and they all laughed.

They got married and lived happily ever after.

****

The story ended, leaving me in tears and a smile on my face, that wasn't willing to fade. Good stories touches your heart, but the best stories touches your soul. This story touched the heart of my soul! I wanted to publish this story!

I needed to contact her as I had many questions regarding the story. As I flipped the end pages of the diary, I found something on the second last page:

Karma Did Slap Me Back
-Rishika Anand
9965656565

'Rishika! Whoa! Was all this about her life?' I wondered.

I instantly dialled her number. After a few rings someone said 'Hello'.

'Hey, is this Rishika?'

"Yes. Who are you?' I realized that the voice wasn't coming from over the phone, but from around me. I turned back and saw her standing, behind me.

''Have a seat, have a seat!'', I hurried.

''I will. But first answer me, why did you touch my diary. Diaries are meant to be personal'' she sighed, exasperated.

"I can publish your story, if you'd let me have the pleasure of asking me some questions", I offered her the diary with a smile.

"What? Seriously? But if you're trying to fool me, then…"

She stopped as I showed her my card with "Rishabh Publishing Club" printed in block letters.

"Sir, I'm sorry. I had been struggling for too long, but every one of them rejected the story because of the homosexual context. Sir I'm telling you India may be developing economically but not mentally."

She sighed with relief, and I noticed her eyes glistening with tears.

"Was this your story?"

She cocked her head to one side, and sighed.

"Sadly, yes."

"Okay! But how did you get to know what happened to Karuna later on", I enquired.

"Sir, the previous year I got a call. With the utterance of just a 'Hello', I recognised it was her. We chatted for a while and planned a meeting. She then recounted what more happened in her life. When she told me she got married, I wasn't hurt. I felt happy for her, I felt like I had been forgiven by the Almighty for atleast 0.1% percent of my sins", she said with a smile full of regrets.

"But… From where did she get your number?"

"I never changed my number since the darkest day of my life."

I got all the answers. We then shook hands as a sign of finalization of the deal.

****

Prachi Priyanka

Dr. Prachi Priyanka is the Creative Head at *Morsels & Juices*. She holds a doctorate degree in English literature and conducts creative writing workshops for young learners. She enjoys weaving articles on various topics – ranging from art criticism to book reviews and relationships to recipes. Prachi is a contributing author in three short story anthologies: *Crumpled Voices, Mighty Thoughts* and *The Zest of Inklings*.

Her articles, stories and poems have been published on several online magazines and journals. She writes with equal ease in English as well as Hindi and her works are published in both the languages. Conflicts and contradictions that emerge in human relationships fascinate her to the core; and her writings are often spilled with varying shades of experiences that intrigue her.

She is a fun-loving person blessed with beautiful family and a bunch of good friends. She likes to learn languages, read books, write blogs, watch movies, experiment art, enjoy cooking, make memories and stay happy.

5

LOVE @ COOKERY CLASS

Prachi Priyanka

They tell her that the way to a man's heart is through his stomach. They tell her many other ways as well – but whatever she tried, she was not able to touch his heart! Now her mother was here to convince her to join a cookery class in the neighborhood. Ma had a valid point though – the classes would keep her engaged throughout the day and leave her with little time to brood on the unending emptiness that surrounded her.

Rupa turned to face the window, avoiding any direct eye contact with Ma. Her eyes had turned moist and a melancholic smile rested lazily on her face – Ma was bright, cheerful and animated; quite unlike her – uneasy and suspicious like some tethered animal sensing a storm. She smiled wistfully as she listened to Ma telling her that if she met people on coffee and went shopping on weekends; she might be happier? "How, Ma? How? She wanted to ask, "Will those people take away my pain and bring my husband back home? Will all the shopping bags weigh more than the heaviness that sinks in my heart as I watch that man spend all his love and attention on that dumb secretary of his?"

Ma spoke in a softer voice now, as if she had read her mind.

"Look Rupa, one doesn't stay in a marriage for love. In most marriages, love vanishes into thin air – sooner or later."

Rupali looked at her mother over her wire-rimmed glasses that had slipped too far down her nose.

Her mother moved a little closer and said animatedly, "What actually keeps a couple glued together is a matter of habit. Habits die hard, you know - and they keep marriages going. Sometimes, for years, even after you fall out of love!"

Rupa smiled inwardly, 'Ma will not give up,' she thought, 'she will try all the tact required to fulfil the undertaken mission; to cajole me to come out of the confines of my comfortable house and step into the outside world.' Ma always had her own logics and arguing with her meant that you choose to fall into her trap. But to join cookery classes was simply out of question. 'Does Ma not know that I have never been enthusiastic about learning to cook and that cooking never found a high rank on my wish list?'

In fact, these days she was not interested in anything – maybe she was dull and frigid, as Rahul said. She wiped her tears and tried to explain her situation to her mother but the way Ma pleaded earnestly on the name of her love for her late father; she was left with no choice but to respect her sentiments.

"Thank you my darling! This is the last time I am asking you to do something for my sake, I promise." Ma said bringing out all her emotions.

"Please Ma, stop being so filmy!" She said to make the conversation lighter.

The last time! Huh! She remembered how her mother had resorted to the same tactics when she was not willing to budge. She had sent them on a vacation to Goa and Rahul couldn't refuse her out of politeness, but what had happened? He had intentionally planned some conferences in the city and chose to either stay out of the room to attend official calls or else bring the work to the hotel room. Rupali had to spend most of her time alone – walking on the beach watching the beautiful sunset or going for some window shopping. But who could make her mother understand that relationships were built not on strategies, but on love. And relationships survived not on habits, but on trust. She knew that Ma wanted to save her marriage. At all cost. She didn't want her daughter to struggle for a living or have to live with the stain of being a divorcee. She wanted to protect her from the prying eyes of lusty men, the questioning glances of relatives and the loneliness that she had to go through when she had become a widow in her early thirties. And so she came up with funny ideas to save her daughter's marriage. Once she had even ventured out into a lingerie store and come with some fancy-looking ones and instructed her in a grave voice, "Try these Rupa. You must not look so plain. If you don't interest him, it is not his fault entirely. You hardly take care of yourself."

That night when Rupa took shower before going to bed, she put on a peach-coloured negligee and looked at herself in the dressing mirror. She looked beautiful. The peach colour of the material matched her complexion. She dabbed some moisturizer all over her body and was about to hug the new Rupa, when Rahul walked into the room. He stared at her bare inviting arms and the low neckline of the dress which stopped just a little below her knees to reveal her smooth, creamy legs. The kind of looks he gave made her immediately regret having agreed to wear it.

"You don't have to do all this, Rupa! Don't you know I feel *nothing* for you?"

She could discern resentment in his voice, as he marched out of their bedroom, crushing her hopes under his feet. Like a fragile strand of sugar syrup, the feeble thread of hope had collapsed upon itself. She kept her eyes lowered as he grumbled, "You know that I love Julie and will not leave her. The sooner you accept this fact – it would be good for both of us."

She had quietly changed to her regular night dress, curled on her side of double bed and let the pillow soak in her sorrow.

She had not told her mother about this episode. She had not told her mother about many other things. She had not told her mother that it was over between them. She had mentioned it once, very casually, that Rahul planned to shift into his office guest house and drop in only to take his belongings or check if she was fine. But she did not have the heart to tell her widowed mother that her daughter's life was destined to be lonely like hers – as Rahul had already signed the divorce papers and sent it to her.

Overwhelmed by her emotions, she instructed herself to forget it all. But her thoughts wouldn't relent, clinging to her like parasites, feeding on her insecurities, her anger and the looming loneliness. They engulfed her, sapping her of all her energy, as if she were drowning in a sad, confusing dream sucking her into its vortex.

How she wanted to hold Ma and share her grief; tell her that she was shattered and that there was no hope to cling on. But then, some things are so difficult.

She went to the washroom, washed her face, treated her swollen eyes with cream and came back to have lunch with her mother and agreeing finally to enrol for the cookery class.

Her mother called up *Tara's Cookery Classes* before Rupa could change her mind and got her enrolled for the next batch. "The classes begin from tomorrow. Three days a week. Be there at ten in the morning. Each session is for two hours. Have your breakfast before you leave home." She continues in an accusing tone, "Now, don't make a face and just sit idly there looking out of the window. It's time to come out and get on with your life. You have been neglecting yourself for too long. Go and check your wardrobe if you have something decent to wear. Or we can go shopping this weekend. I can always spare a few hours for you." Ma said with a tinge of eagerness.

"Ma, I will manage. I have enough in the wardrobe. And I am not going to attend a wedding that you are getting so anxious. It is just a cookery class in the locality. What is the big deal?"

"Ok fine. You'll thank me one day for coming up with this proposal. But anyways, for the time being, I thank you for being a good daughter and listening to your Ma. Take care Rupa, I will call you tomorrow evening."

"I'll call you Ma, thanks for coming. And you take care too."

****

"Sorry Ma, I slept in the afternoon. So missed your calls." She said apologetically, voice still sounding sleepy.

"You must have been tired dear. I called to ask how your first day was."

"It was good, Ma. Today, Tara basically introduced herself and spent most of the time promoting her cookbooks – when, where and how you can buy them etc. and then she talked about the important role food plays in our lives."

A smile spreads on her face as it flashed to her that the ease of familiarity with which Tara bonded with them felt nice. She carried herself with seamless grace and a welcoming smile as she gave a brief introduction about the class.

"So, how many of you are here to impress your spouse with your culinary skills?" Tara had asked, sweeping the whole class with a glance.

A few hands rose.

Rupa had felt it embarrassing to make a public confession of what was her mother's silly idea to win a man. But Tara seemed to belong to the same school of thinking for her next sentence was,

"Men have only two emotions – hungry or horny. So, if sex is not on his mind, make him a sandwich." Tara winked and watched some women laugh out loud, while others broke in suppressed giggles.

Though amused, Rupa felt herself too stiff to smile. She buried herself into the small recipe booklet that was handed over to them when they came to the class. During the break hour, women exchanged conversations that jumped from pictures of recipes to parenting woes and ended with proffering advice on the best tailors in town.

"What happened? Why are you so silent?" Her mother got restless on the other side of phone.

"I am okay Ma."

"You did not tell me how many women are there in your batch?"

"We are ten, Ma." She said briefly.

She counted in her head once again. There were four women who came from a nearby locality. Two of them were sister-in-laws who said they wanted to open their own cookery classes; the other two women wanted to learn new dishes and earn applauds on their next Ladies' Kitty. Then there was the middle-aged Dolly, who seemed to be good at cooking and Rupa rather found it annoying the way she was being preachy about it. Her partner, Jaya, hardly spoke, and rarely participated in group talks. Dolly told them that Jaya was keen on learning how to bake pizzas and cakes. And finally they had a lovey-dovey couple who exchanged furtive glances during the class, rejoicing in the company of each other. The wife told them that she was here to learn some basic cooking but it was entirely her husband's idea to take a half-day leave from office and join her in the classes.

"So will you get to do some cooking yourselves?" Her mother enquired.

"Yes Ma. From our next class, we are to work in groups of two. We will cover a range of recipes and will be learning about the dishes in one session and try cooking them ourselves in the other."

"Sounds good."

"Hmmm"

She did not tell Ma that she was paired with a *firangi*. She was late to the class and had quietly sat on a corner chair next to this man. Tara had asked each one to work in pairs, which had led to a lot of commotion in the room - shifting of chairs and excited voices. She, for once felt like running away from all this chaos when she had heard him say, "Hi, I am Alex – from London."

It had fascinated her the way he waved his arms about as he talked. Even the halting accent seemed cute to her.

"Hi, I am Rupali. I live in the neighbourhood." She had replied after a longish pause.

Alex told her that he was in India for the last one year. That he was writing a book on the culture and cuisine of India and was here to attend this cookery class to get a basic idea of the preferences of Indian taste in food.

She did not know how to explain why she was here. The same way that she did not know how her mother would react if she told her that for the next thirty or more classes, she will be stuck with a young aspiring British author whom she found appealing.

The next day she reached class on time. They greeted each other when their eyes met. For most of the time, however, they had to listen to the instructor's guidelines on Indian cooking which was followed by step-wise demonstration of a recipe. They were advised to note down the highlights in their diaries. Rupa was already yawning. This was her time to take a nap after her eyes would tire themselves watching the repeat shows of daily soaps. Much against her will, she took down notes on how to make *jalebis* at home. Something she never intended to take the trouble of doing, especially when they were easily accessible in every sweet shop.

Much without her anticipation, Tara provided them with required ingredients and asked them to make *jalebis* without taking assistance from their recipe diaries. Rupa could not recall the measurements of the ingredients – or the exact process to be followed. It added to her misery when Alex looked at her expectantly: "Have you made *Jalebis* before?"

"Nope." She shrugged her shoulders to pull down any hope that he might have been building on her.

"Same here." He grinned.

His face was suddenly transformed, taking it straight from looking aloof and condescending to a naughty boyish look. She volunteered to help but to a little effect. Their dish turned out to be a complete fiasco and Tara warned them to be more attentive next time. Rupa felt bad for Alex. It wasn't his fault that she was yawning in class yesterday while others jotted down the details of *jalebi*-making. Besides, Alex had reluctantly told her that the batter looked thinner than what the instructor had prepared in the demonstration class, but the poor guy had trusted her more than his own memory. Therefore, in the break-time, Rupa decided to make-up for spoiling the recipe by buying a packet of freshly-made *jalebis* for Alex.

"What's this?" Alex asked surprised.

"*Jalebis*. Enjoy!" She answered him with a smile.

"Have them. I bought them from the shop you see in that corner." She pointed her finger towards the direction of the shop. "Look, this is my way to say sorry. Now, have them please." He laughed and picked up a piece of jalebi.

"Yup, they are really nice - though a bit sweet for me!" There was good humour gleaming in his rat-like eyes, which twinkled when he smiled.

She offered *jalebis* to other participants as well and it felt good to meet new people. Ma was right. It was a welcome change from being numbed by vein-scrapping boredom that came from indulging in silly soap operas and bad comedies on television.

Life had changed considerably for her these days. She woke up early and worked hard to finish the chores on time. After coming back from class, she would take a nap. Evenings, however, were dull - mostly spent talking to Ma on phone or sometimes going out to buy the essentials for home. She has stopped waiting for Rahul to help her with the shopping.

There was one more change that she had added to her life style. She found it funny that after a long time she was trying out new recipes at home. It filled her with immense satisfaction when the dish turned out to be good enough to eat and therefore, sometimes she would save a little to share with the cookery class friends – a beautiful change after all these months of lonely meals in the cramped stillness of sadness. It was not just food but a part of their own lives that they shared with one another. A new world seemed unfold before her slowly. Listening to sad experiences of other people and the way they dealt with the troubles in life gives her a chance to look beyond her own dreams and despair. To earn her husband's love and attention and save their tattered marriage had come to occupy so important a place in her three years of married life that she cared little to connect with people or think beyond her own challenges. She had a reasonably good academic background but in all these years of depression, she had not cared to develop any hobby or career that could give a dimension to her personality and add to some sense of fulfilment in life.

Earlier weekends used to be tiring and long, but not anymore. She would visit her mother on Saturdays and on her way back, stopped to buy groceries. Rahul's car would be parked outside at times; they would greet each other and sip tea in between polite conversations. This time she did not poke him about his secretary or persuade him to stay a little longer when he would want to leave. She would go to see him off to the car in a composed demeanour.

He would ask, "Would you need the car? Now that you go out more often."

"Thanks Rahul. But no. I'll manage. And I don't travel far." She would say it, with a new found freedom in her own voice.

Rahul certainly looked surprised at this change. He smiled. "Bye then. Take care!"

******

On a Sunday morning, Rupa was surprised to receive a call from Alex. Yes, they had exchanged phone numbers, but she had never expected him to call her. He asked if she could give him company to tour the city. She could easily have refused but part of her was excited about the thought of going out of the house. Wherever it be.

They spend the entire afternoon on the streets of Delhi. Rupa had not walked so much in a day.

"I would love to know more about the ancient and medieval structures and their ruins. Your country has a rich heritage."

She smiled with pride.

"It would be silly to ask, knowing that you are a local – but have you seen Qutub Minar?"

"I have. But it has been a long time. Probably the last time I went to the place, I was in college."

They loitered for long at the Qutub complex area. Guides talking in broken English surrounded Alex like flies. They hired a guide to navigate through their culture's past and talked about the interesting facets of the country's tallest Minar. Alex collected a few pamphlets from the enquiry office and dug the guide questions to understand the Islamic inscriptions inscribed on the monument. He clicked photos of the Minar from different angles and sometimes shot her, completely rapt in her own thoughts.

"Please don't click me. I am not photogenic." She said lamely.

"Don't worry! I am good behind the lens." He smiled and showed her snaps of hers, he had just taken, against the backdrop of the monument.

"Yes, this is really pretty!"

"And so are you!" he winked at her and took her hand, "come on, let's find a decent place to have lunch. You must be hungry!"

She did not hear his words. All she knew was that it felt good to walk hand in hand, making way through the crawling crowd. She had never walked like this with Rahul, or anyone.

"I was right. You are too hungry to talk or even smile back!"

"No Alex, I am fine. Just was thinking something."

He spotted a restaurant.

"What do you think so much Rupa? One moment you are with me, another, you are lost! Why so?" He asked after placing their orders.

"You have become Mona Lisa for me. What is it that you are hiding behind your evasive smiles? Won't you share?" He looked straight into her eyes.

There was something in his voice, in the way he looked – that urged her to open up before him. She told him briefly about the turbulent phase that her marriage was going through and how her mother had coaxed her into joining the cookery class. He listened to her with the kind of attention one devotes when reading a dictionary and as she travelled back to the miserable years of her life with Rahul, all of a sudden he asked "Voila! Would you like to co-author my book?"

She looked blankly at him.

"What? You didn't like the idea?"

"No, it's not that, Alex." She smiled. "I don't have any idea about writing a book! I have never given a thought to it."

"Then give it a thought. We can together work on it. Listen, I intend to cover the ancient monuments, the early paintings and the stories behind them. If you are willing, I can guide you on how to proceed. You'll find it exciting I bet!"

She was already excited. And also scared at the sudden steep turns her life was taking.

She kept turning sides the whole night. Nascent dreams took away sleep from her eyes.

The next day she went to meet her mother after class. Her mother is surprised to see her on a weekday.

"How are your classes going, Rupa?"

"Nice Ma, it finishes in two weeks now. I plan to enrol myself for the next session as well."

"That's good. I like your spirit girl." She kissed her on the forehead like she always did when she got emotional.

"Nice dress! Is it new?" she asked admiringly, looking closely at the fabric of her skirt.

"Yes Ma, bought it last week. You know, my wardrobe was full of all junk." She laughed as she said.

"You look good in skirt dear. You should wear it more often!" Rupa glowed with happiness.

She loved the fragrance of incense sticks that Ma lit every day, the ash coloured, and Jasmine scented smoke pervaded the room and relaxed her mind.

After lunch they relaxed in her mother's room. An enormous black and white photograph of her deceased father hung near the door. She had seen her mother wipe her tears and speak to the picture.

The November heat filtered in from the glass window and filled the place with an idle drowsiness. Rupa curled herself on bed, positioned her head on her mother's lap and dropped in the idea of writing a travel book with Alex, the guy she had met at the cookery classes.

Ma sat straight on the bed, looking suspiciously at her. "So this is it? You were going around with that *firangi* these days! This is what you are cooking at your cookery classes! Shame, Rupa!"

Rupa looked horrified at her mother. She knew Ma was vocal about her opinions and prejudiced at times, but now it filled her with a remote sense of resentment for her. The sunlight grew brutal and blinding. She had always stopped herself from sharing with Ma anything about Alex. She had not told her that she liked to buy jalebis for him only to see the twinkle in his eyes; that she had spent many lonely evenings thinking of him; and that even a casual compliment from him made her blush. She was in a mix of conflicting emotions. How could Ma know her heart so well and yet fail to understand how she felt?

"And I'm sure he has bought you this dress too?"

"Stop it Ma. I am not a thirteen year old girl that you are prying on. Why would he buy me a dress? You are being ridiculous! Weaving stories out of nothing! It was my fault that I thought I should consult you before getting into this venture of book writing."

Ma would definitely return to the topic of the dress. But for the time being she shifted the focus of her argument. "But why book writing? You have done a teacher's training course. So why not join some school and live a life of respect."

"I might join a school some time, Ma. But not now. I want to explore the city. Learn new things myself before I settle to teach others. Try to understand, Ma."

"But you hardly know the guy! Or anything about his background, his family, his upbringing! How can you trust him?"

"*Trust?*" she laughs as if it's a joke. "You knew Rahul's family so well. We were family friends for three decades. I wanted to continue my studies, but it was you who cajoled me to marry him – on *trust*. But what happened, Ma? Rahul had a girlfriend and he was afraid to *trust* his parents to tell them about her! And imagine, he *trusts* me – and decides to share his love life on our first night! I loved him, and kept his secret to myself. For several months, I kept pretending that everything was alright between us – till you discovered about that girl and questioned him and his parents. And what did it all lead to? His parents left him, he left me and I now live alone in that big house."

She said it firmly and then bursts into tears. Her mother's anger had vanished. She stroked Rupa's head slowly and said in a comforting tone, "Everything will be alright my love. Don't worry. He will come back to you. He is just a little distracted. Nothing else!"

Distracted!

"Ma, for God's sake he is not distracted! He doesn't love me. He never did. He is to marry his girlfriend soon. So stop pretending that everything will be alright. It's over. But let's wish the best for him. Please Ma, it's time to move on."

******

She ran a high temperature after she was back from her mother's place. She informed Tara that she would not be able to attend classes for a week. Ma did not call her after all the arguments they had in their previous meeting. She got up to cook something for herself, when the doorbell rang.

It was Alex.

After the initial conversations he enquired if she was taking medicines and meals on time. And when she fumbled for words, he found his way to her kitchen despite her protests and came out with something in a bowl.

"Here, have the soup." he said in a matter-of-fact tone. She quietly gulped in a few spoons of it and then weakly stretched her legs a little and slept on the sofa, crumpled up like some drained wineskin.

He sat by her bedside, stroking her head, sifting her hair through his fingers, letting the strands glide effortlessly like penguins on ice.

When Rupa opened her eyes wearily; she found him sitting by her side, waiting to give her medicines before he left for the day and promised to be there again the next day. Every time he did something for her; she had to try hard to keep her loud breathing bottled inside her chest.

"You have a big house." He said one day, as his eyes travellev around the room.

"It's not *mine*. It is my husband's." She said after a pause, "I plan to shift in some rented accommodation next month."

"Oh, I see." He smiled, with sort of a golden glow that spread over his round, pinkish face.

He insisted to come on the weekend, though she assured him that she was perfectly well. During lunch, their conversations gravitated towards their own countries, their families and finally the book.

"I don't know how to thank you Alex for all that you have done." She said, feeling obliged.

"Accept my proposal then."

When her eyes widened in surprise and she fluttered down in confusion, her face a curious mix of awkwardness and anticipation, he laughed and clarified, "I was talking about our book?"

So he had been serious about the idea of sharing the authorship with her.

"Anything for you!" she murmured gratefully.

"Anything? Ah! Are you sure?" he winked and took her hand.

The sun poured through the windows, filtering gently through the curtains that shimmered in the glow of newly felt warmth.

His smile gathered her in a warm embrace. Life had never felt so beautiful to Rupa.

Brinda Tailor

Brinda Tailor is a 19 years old student, born and brought up in Bharuch, Gujarat. She is currently in second year pursuing electronics & communication degree from DDIT. She started writing poems at the age of 15. After realizing her keen interest in writing, she started writing blog, poems, short stories and notes. 'A Night in Paradise' is her first attempt in writing a fictional short story, in that sense it is her literary debut. As her name 'Brinda' means 'Tulsi', so is her passion to serve humanity. She is a very chirpy, lovable and caring person. She values her relations with friends and family high, above all. Besides writing, she is highly passionate about photography and handles the camera very well. Her friends call her camera her 'soul mate'. Her love for sports makes her a very good volley ball player. In her spare time, she loves listening music to sharpen her creative ability. Her other anthologies as a contributing author are Life Sundae, Goofy, 31 Sins, Crumpled Voices 2. She is one of the compliers of the Anthology 'Snowflakes of Love'.

She can be contacted at: brindatailor@gmail.com

Facebook: www.facebook.com/brindatailor

Milan Modi

Milan Modi, from Gujarat, is an engineering student. He took to writing after winning essay writing competitions at school. He maintains a blog by the name 'hidden-treasure.blogspot.com' He has also contributed a short story to an anthology named, 'Life Sundae.' He loves playing cricket & snooker and believes in taking up any challenge in life.

You can reach him at -milanmodi94@gmail.com

Facebook connect: www.facebook.com/modimilanrocks

6

THE BELOVED CRUSH

Milan Modi & Brinda Tailor

It was 60' clock in the morning and the atmosphere was calm. There was dead silence all over, not even the sound of snoring was heard. The noise of the alarm broke the deep sleep of Aditi's dad. He woke up, went to his daughter's room to wake her up for studying. He opened the door of her room and went near her, gently placed his hand on her forehead and said "Aditi, beta, wake up or else you won't be able to follow your schedule."

"Yes dad five more minutes." She said in a sleepy voice.

"Okay, will wake you up in five minutes!" his dad said and left her room.

Her bed was neat and perfectly made. Her room had more shelves of books than the cupboards of clothes. She was not like other girls, or she was told not to be like other girls.

Aditi looked graceful. Her hair falling on her shoulders and for most of the time, tied in a hair band with bow stuck on it. She was so busy with her studies that she did not pay much attention to her girly needs. She never made any friend with boys. Her beautiful brown eyes were hidden behind her huge spectacles that gave a bookworm types look. She was a bookworm indeed!

Aditi woke up and sat on the bed, extended her hand towards the table that was beside her. She picked up her rectangle framed spectacles that were quite big for her face. She totally looked like a nerd with those huge glasses, but she was beautiful.

"So beta, what's the target today? How many pages to mug up?" her mom said entering the room with a glass full of Bournvita.

"Don't know mom, jitna hoga utna." She said uninterestedly as she slurped the chocolate milk.

"3 chapters. Okay?" her mom asked. Her eyes questioned.

"Mom this is 11th class, not the board exams!" Aditi said, a bit tensed.

Her mom left the room.

She wished to announce; *'I don't like studying; all I want to do is study LITERATURE, not MEDICAL.'*

She was upset with the circumstances in her life. Getting good grades didn't mean you want to take medical. Her parents did not give her a chance to think and announced that she was going to study medicine.

'What about my wish? Isn't it my life?' she questioned herself.

She always ended up asking the same question again and again to herself, which she knew she won't be able to answer. It killed her every time when she saw someone reading a novel or doing poetry work.

Penning down her feelings into words was her favorite hobby.

Alas! Her parents didn't allow it. They belonged to the typical conservative family, who wanted their daughter to be a doctor and not something like a struggler in writing field. She used to pen down her feelings whenever she was left alone. It was not like she hated studying, but she didn't want to become a doctor.

She just started scrolling the book page by page mugging up, grasping it line by line. The way all the bookworms read, she was no different.

Finishing her part of that day, she closed the book like somebody banging a door in anger.

Collecting herself, she got ready for her school.

Two pony tails, big spectacle, a bag loaded with lots of books. She looked like a perfect bookworm.

As soon she entered the classroom, Shikha tapped her from behind saying

"Hey Einstein, where are you going?"

Shikha was her childhood friend or say her only friend in the whole class. She was totally different from Aditi. She had a care-free attitude towards everything, unlike Aditi. Many times her parents gave her advice to become like Aditi and score good marks but she never cared to listen, whereas Aditi wanted to become carefree like Shikha.

"Going to library, where else?" Aditi replied taking her pen out.

"Okay, me too going there. C'mon lets go together." Shika replied and started moving towards library.

As usual Aditi was busy taking notes from the various books written by some of the doctors for her biology project.

"Come Aditi, look at this poster." Shikha exclaimed in excitement.

Aditi ignored her, thinking it to be yet another prank to distract her.

"Come fast Aditi, I am serious this time." Shikha yelled again.

The whole library stared at them furiously.

Looking at everybody's reaction, Aditi closed her book and went towards Shikha.

"What is your problem? Don't you know this is library? Can't you behave yourself?" Aditi started scolding her.

As soon as her lecture got over, Shikha turned Aditi's face towards the window wall. A big poster was clipped to it.

It read-

"Buddy magazine by the students of class 11thA.

Any types of entries are considered according to the sections.

EDITED BY- SIDDARTH MALHOTRA."

Aditi continued to look in the poster.

"He is so hot and handsome". Shikha said in a seductive tone seeing Siddarth's photo.

"Na, he looks like a monkey." Aditi answered.

"What you know about boys ha? Every girl is dying to be his girlfriend." Shikha backfired in a loud voice.

That time she was right. Aditi never had any male friend. She had only been with Shikha from the very start. She hardly even spoke to any boy.

Actually she never got time to talk to boys or flirt with them. Her parents were her guidance and books and pen were her best friends.

"I know you write poems and thoughts and keep them hidden from everyone and even from me." Shikha said. This time, calmly.

"I don't want to read them but want you to write for this magazine.

Shikha explained her care for Aditi's writing.

"No. Who told you that I write?" Aditi replied roughly trying to hide the truth.

All her efforts went vain, when Shikha took out a diary from Aditi's bag.

"Beta, I am your best friend. I know everything." Shikha said looking at Aditi's insecurity.

"Let's go from here, I have completed my notes." Aditi replied trying to change the topic.

"He's too hot. You have to write an article so that I can get in touch with him." Shikha said winking at Aditi.

The whole day was monotonous for her. Even in the night, her parents pressurized her to mug up things and the notes she took in the day. She was too frustrated with all this.

Suddenly she remembered that Shikha took a photograph of the magazine poster from her cell phone.

She started seeing the different topics, but didn't have guts to write for them as it would create a forest fire at her house if they came to know.

She just closed everything and banged the books and slept.

"Aditi come on wake up. We need to rush."

Aditi woke up trying to find what happened, grabbed her spectacle and saw Shikha neatly dressed in school uniform.

"What happened? It's still 6 o'clock. Why are you so early? Aditi questioned cleaning her eyes.

"I knew you will forget that today is our extra lecture. Now be ready in ten minutes."

Even her parents were happy to see Shikha's sincerity.

"Which extra lecture you are talking about?"

"I will tell you on the way. Now please get ready."

After fifteen minutes Shikha and Aditi reached the school. Shikha went directly towards library and asked Aditi to follow her. Aditi had no clue why she was at school when nobody else had shown up. As soon as Aditi entered, she was shocked to see Shikha talking to the same person who was in the poster a day prior.

"Hey Sid, she's my best friend, Aditi whom I was talking about. She wants to write for your magazine." Shikha said introducing Aditi.

"That's great. I should enroll her name in the list." Sid replied taking out a paper.

Aditi was looking Sid without blinking!

"Mam, can I have your name and address?" Sid asked Aditi to complete the details.

Aditi was dumbstruck. She even didn't move and kept gazing at Sid. Shikha tapped her from behind and asked her to reply to him.

It seemed like Sid had done some magical spell on her. She never felt like this for anyone. As soon as she gave the necessary details, they went from there.

Aditi was still bound to that atmosphere. Yes! She had fallen for him. It was clearly visible from her reaction.

All her anger for Shikha melted down and was converted into a beautiful smile. She thanked Shikha.

"I hope you won't have a crush on him?" Shikha inquired, trying to know what happened in the library.

"No re, nothing like that. Don't think useless things." Aditi replied furiously looking at Shikha.

But from inside she knew that she was lying. She did feel something. An adrenaline rush was flowing in her veins. She didn't know what was happening to her.

Coming to the class, she again saw Sid. She felt butterflies in her stomach. The whole day went by just like that!

At night, again the same schedule followed and her frustration grew more.

Suddenly her cell vibrated. She picked the phone and it was a message. It read:

"Hi."

She was confused and replied.

"Who's this and how did you get my number?"

In flash of a second it vibrated again.

"This is Sid, got your number from the registration form. Hope you don't mind. Shikha told me that you are shy and so wanted to ask if you need any help with writing."

Aditi was in seventh heaven. She was thinking about him only before he had texted.

"Not a problem, I'll manage it Siddharth." she replied to the text hiding her excitement and hidden feelings.

This conversation went on and on. She didn't know she slept.

Next morning, she was full of energy. Now she desperately wanted to go to school. They both didn't know when they started talking regularly till late nights. Aditi started sharing anything and everything with him. Sid silently listened to her and helped her to make her smile in the worst moments. Sid knew about her parents and all the tortures she had to go with everyday.

An insecurity feeling started to come up whenever Aditi used to see him talking to some other girl or even Shikha. She didn't know what was happening to her but she didn't want to lose him by sharing her feelings her him. This was totally new for her. Shikha started to smell something fishy within her.

The sudden shyness, the hidden excitement, the insecurity was all over her. Her crush feelings had started to convert into something special called love. She always felt frightened to talk about her feelings.

Days passed and their exams came nearer. She started spending most of her time with her books. Whole day she used to study and then used to talk to Sid till midnight.

A night before the exam, Aditi called him but found his number busy. It gave a terrified feeling to her. She was unable to concentrate on the revision and the whole night she just kept on staring at her cell phone to the only photo that she had of him.

Next day she entered the examination hall but she was not the same that she used to be. She didn't even open her book. Her eyes were continuously trying to find Sid and she didn't bother to read the question paper.

Finally she found him, sitting on the last bench, kneeling his head down. A smile was exchanged by both of them and Sid signaled her to write. This was the only thing she wanted. She wanted someone to be there for her. Somehow she managed to write the paper.

During the nights, she would desperately try to call him, but would always get a busy tone or switched-off message. She would try to explain herself that, he must be buys studying.

She wanted to cry aloud with her heart, but there was no one around to listen. Somehow she managed to give the exams, but she didn't do well in that.

Exams got over and she was afraid to face her biggest fear - RESULT. She knew that her parents were surely going to be mad at her. She needed someone to sooth her, stop her tears and hug her, she needed Siddharth.

On the other side, he was unaware of all the things happening to Aditi. The night passed and the sun rose. She did not feel any 'ray of hope' but the 'light before darkness' hovered over her mind. Her eyes got swollen because of lack of sleep and vigorous crying.

She got ready and went to school for taking the report card. Her eyes still searching for her guy and as usual she found him talking to some other girl of her class.

"It's hard to digest when your feelings get crushed by your own crush." She thought.

In no time, her result was in her hand. She knew it was going to be bad but it turned out to be horrible. It seemed to be the worst day of her life. She hardly passed in all the subjects and got C grade. It pricked her heart seeing Sid flirting with someone else and her heart got totally crushed due to her results.

When her parents asked for her result, she handed it to them. Land slipped below their feet. Their eyes got stuck in that piece of paper. They could hardly believe what they saw. All their dreams came to an end when they saw her result. Their anger was at the peak. Everything was falling apart for her. Her parents made her life worse.

They didn't beat her up but their cruel words were enough to kill her mentally. They even told her to leave their house, if she didn't become a doctor. Many restrictions were put on her. She hardly spoke to anybody.

Going to school and coming back to home become a job for her. She daily saw Sid but didn't have guts to speak about her feelings. The torture kept on increasing as her relatives came to know. It worked like a fuel in the deadly fire that was destroying her life.

Shikha too got busy in her life. Her only friend was her love for writing. She kept on writing about the dark and tortuous nights of her life. It was getting tough for her to go on with her life.

It was not like she didn't wanted to live, but living like this felt meaningless to her. She just penned down her feelings for Sid. She didn't have any clue when her crush got converted into love.

"Tring, tring".

Shikha picked her cell phone up, which was continuously ringing since fifteen minutes.

Aditi was there on the other side. Shikha was in deep sleep. She hardly could open her eyes.

"Hello, what happened Aditi? Why you are awake this late?"

Shikha said in a voice indicating that she was angry to get awake this late.

"I need you to do me a favor. Please collect an article from my home tomorrow and deliver it to Sid for his magazine. I won't be coming to school tomorrow."

Aditi described the reason for calling in one breath. "Okay, I will." Shikha replied and disconnected the phone without even asking what the matter was.

After she hung up, Aditi tried to think about her life that was now being controlled by her parents. She tried to think about gaining back her freedom. The only thought came to her was to leave her house.

Tears were rolling down her eyes and simultaneously she was packing her bag. She tried to stuff every possible thing she could. She tried to accommodate maximum clothes in her school bag with a few papers and a pen.

All she was now searching for was 'freedom.' She tried to comfort herself on the bed and sleep, but she was lost in the deep thoughts of her love and was unable to sleep. That night she lied on the bed with her eyes wide open.

Next morning, Shikha collected the article and went to school.

She was very much excited to read that but Aditi had sealed the paper in an envelope. Aditi had also texted Sid to collect the envelope from Shikha. Shikha was unable bear the curiosity so she broke the seal and a piece of paper with beautiful decorations came out.

It read

"THE SECRET CRUSH"

Crushes are the most awesome thing in this world full of betrayals, backstabbing and heartbreaks. Crush is that feeling between the pure love and friendship.

You don't know whether you see your future with them or not. Whether they feel the same way as you feel. You just stupidly smile when they are near you and become sad for no reason if they don't talk to you in the whole day. That's why people call it "crush".

You just make them special without any reason. Everything feels just perfect when they are with you without any commitment or any demands. Sometimes I felt the same way with that special one......

"Excuse me?" May I get the envelope?" Sid said and saw Shikha peeping in the envelope. Sid interrupted Shikha in between the article.

"Ya take this."

She spoke handing it over to him while he kept grinning at her silly act.

"Thank you."

He said and left the place.

Sikha was almost about to reach the best part but couldn't do anything.

Sid reached the library and took out the envelope. He was curious and excited at the same time. As soon as he completed reading the article, he ran towards the exit without saying a word to anybody. He knew the article was for him.

He directly went to Aditi's home. He was just thinking of Aditi the entire time on his way to her home. How Aditi used to share everything with him. Even he also felt the same way but didn't take it seriously. Every single meeting of them was flashing in his mind.

Thinking of her, he reached her home.

"Aditi,"aditi".

He shouted from outside the lane. Her parents came and told him that she is at school. Sid knew something was fishy because Shikha had already told him that Aditi won't be coming to school today.

He rushed to her room without listening to her parents. Finding nobody there and seeing all the things badly messed up, he got furious with anger. All his anger came out at her parents as Sid knew how they tortured her for studies and went outside to find her.

Suddenly, the mobile in Siddhartha's pocket vibrated. It showed an incoming call from an unknown number.

As soon as he picked the call, the lady on the other side inquired "May I talk to Mr. Siddharth Malhotra, its urgent?"

"Yes?" Sid said waiting for the reply. "Sir, I don't know what is your relation with Miss Aditi Singh, but she met with an accident and is in I.C.U. in our hospital. We got to know about your contact number because it was written on a letter that was in her hand. Can you please come here as soon as possible?"

The receptionist of L.D. Hospital informed about Aditi's critical condition.

Sid noted down the address of the hospital and informed about the accident to Aditi's parents, burnt the engine of his bike and headed towards the place. Aditi's parents followed him.

Hurriedly and fearfully they asked the receptionist about Aditi. The nurse took Siddharth and Aditi's parents to her and they saw her lying on the I.C.U. bed. Her parents went to the doctor.

Sid's eyes were full of tears when he saw her unconscious. He tried to control his tears and followed her parents.

"Sir, we found these things with Miss Aditi." A nurse came and extended her hand to give the letter and her bag to Sid.

No sooner did he saw his name on the letter, then he opened it and started reading:

Dear Siddharth,

First of all I would like to apologize for all these things. I never intended to fall in love with the guy I never thought would ever be mine. I don't even know whether you belong with me or not.

Falling for you was never my choice, but now, being in love with you forever is what I chose. Unknowingly, I was in love with you but I never came to know about what I felt.

My heart becomes happy to see you by my side, but it sobs heavily when we fall apart. Being in love with you, makes me feel better than I've ever felt. The way you cared for me, nobody did. The way you understood me gave me courage to live. You are my strongest strength and my weakest weakness. Seeing you smile is all I wanted. I would be glad if the smile would stick on your face forever. I've always loved you, I am still in love with you and I will love you till my death and even after that.

Love, Aditi

Tears roll down his cheeks and he started talking to himself 'How can someone love me so much? I never did anything special for her.'

He regretted not being with her earlier. He started blaming things on himself. He thought all these things were happening because of him.

He rushed towards Aditi's bed, hugged her and started crying again.

"Aditi, I am sorry. Adi, please wake up, see I am there by your side always, please open your eyes and smile just as you always did when you saw me? Please Aditi, don't keep me waiting anymore." he pleaded to the unconscious girl lying on the bed but his efforts went in vain, Aditi was still unconscious.

"Sir, Dr. Kashyap wants to talk to you." the nurse said and pointed Sid to go to the doctor's cabin.

"Yes Dr. Kashyap, I am Siddharth Malhotra, Aditi's friend." Sid said as he signalled him to sit on one of the chair.

"Mr. Siddharth, we did a few tests and the result shows that Aditi has blood clotting in brain, which can completely harm her brain and her entire body. We have done the necessary operations on the external injuries caused by the accident." he said with grief and handed the file of reports to Aditi's parents. They broke into tears.

"Doctor, when will she be alright?" Sid asked with creases on his forehead.

"Soon Mr. Malhotra, just in a month or two, she will be at home. But she needs to be taken care of. She needs rest." The doctor replied.

"Thank god." Sid said with a slight smile, still he was blaming himself for all this things and it was eating him from inside.

"Sir, she has regained consciousness." said a nurse who came running to the cabin.

Everybody got up, Aditi's parents were happy but they didn't know how to face her. They had guilt in their eyes as well as heart. Siddharth hurried to her room and knelt to the floor beside her bed.

"Aditi, why didn't you tell this to me earlier? Why did you do this to yourself? I love you Adi, I love you a lot, promise me that you won't ever leave me."

"Seeing my condition, I can't promise that, I am breathing my last days." Adi tried to speak a bit.

"Why are you making me cry? I know you will be with me forever." Sid said and tried to control the flow.

"I love you Sid, I love you a lot, I don't want to live without you. "She said.

"Adi, I will never let you go." he promised, held her hand tightly and kissed her forehead. The hospital was full of peoples' cries and screams of the patients. Everything seemed so worse and negative vibes were all over there.

"What's the time Sid?" she questioned. "Its 9.30 P.M. sweetie." he answered. "I am just sick of this hospital atmosphere, please take me somewhere else Sid." she requested and tried to get up. "Wait Adi, let me ask the doctor." he said.

Sid went to Dr. Kashyap and asked for his permission to take Aditi out of the hospital.

"Yes sure Mr. Siddharth, there's no harm, but be careful, no stress. She is still in critical state." the doctor signalled.

Sid knew the risk but didn't have the guts to refuse to Aditi's request. Sid came back to the room and tried to dress his hair with his hands. For the first time he was taking his girl out on a date and that too on hospital's terrace.

Sid lifted her in his arms and moved towards the elevator. Smile stuck Aditi's face when they reached upstairs. There was dead silence all over and they could just see the lights of the houses and shops in the city. They sat on one of the corner of the terrace, gazing at the stars. Aditi was leaning on Sid and kept her head on his shoulder and that made her feel complete.

"Aditi, you haven't answered my question yet." Sid said.

"Sid, I never said what I felt for you because I never wanted to lose you. I love you a lot Sid and I will definitely fail to explain my feelings in words. I don't want to die so early Sid; I want to spend the rest of my life with you. But, even if I die today, I will be dying in your arms. So I don't have to worry, I will die with a smile."

She said with tears flowing from her eyes and hugged him.

He held her in his arms, planted a kiss on her cheeks made her feel secure.

"Sid, I am tired, I want to sleep in your arms." she said making herself comfortable. She closed her eyes, smiled and slept listening to the heart beating for her.

The next morning was the most deadly morning when Sid woke and found her dead in his arms. Yes, her heart stopped beating. She made her way to the heaven that night. He didn't believe what he was just seeing. Aditi was lying dead in his arms with a smile. He cried and tried to digest the bitter truth that she was no more.

Her memories played a sweet melody in his mind.

"Love isn't about always being together. It is about loving someone even if you can't be with them."

"Aditi, this was the last line of your article, right? I will always love you Aditi, no matter what." he said bursting out into tears.

Sreelekha Chaterjee

Sreelekha Chatterjee is a researcher and an editor. She has edited several scientific and social science books/journals. Her short stories have been published in a number of anthologies and magazines. She has a postgraduate degree in science from Calcutta University and is also a trained singer with a degree in music (GeetaBharati).

Some of her short stories include 'Wisdom of the Decision' in *Chicken Soup for the Indian Bride's Soul* (Westland Ltd, India, 2011), 'Friendship Beyond Rules and Norms' in *Chicken Soup for the Indian Soul: On Friendship* (Westland Ltd, India, 2011), 'The Direct Approach' in *Wisdom of Our Mothers* (Familia Books, USA, 2012), 'A Sense of Sibling Love' in *Chicken Soup for the Indian Soul: Celebrating Brothers and Sisters* (Westland Ltd, India, 2012), 'Wisdom So Uncommon' in *'Hope': An Anthology of Literary Pieces* (Lituminati, India, 2014), 'The Fatal Pride' in Crumpled Voices: Shades of Suffering (Gargi Publishers, India, 2014) and 'A Sense of Touch' (Femina, India, 2014).

7

BOTH SIDES OF THE STORY

Sreelekha Chaterjee

I was busy with an important experiment in my room when I heard a loud cry. It took a moment for me to realize that the sound was coming from the Chemistry lab. Apart from me, there were two male lab attendants and Reena in the lab. All of us had reached a little earlier than usual to perform our individual duties.

I rushed to the Chemistry lab and found Reena groaning in pain, while blood oozed out from the fingers of her right hand and spattered her workstation and portions of the floor. I was unable to react to the situation, I stood there incapable of moving a limb—flustered and horrified. With great difficulty I collected myself, and took her in my arms. She let herself loose, sliding freely up against my chest like an innocent child looking for comfort in a mother's embrace. Her tears mingled with blood smudged on my white apron, determined to leave a mark of the shocking and unfortunate episode. I wiped her tears that were streaming down her helpless eyes, and tried to console her by uttering the usual words, 'everything will be fine.' She clutched my hands with a strange fierceness and kept on saying, 'I'm going to die.'

Being the only senior member present in the lab at that hour, I had to instruct the lab attendants to call the emergency service of the company. An ambulance reached the lab almost immediately in response to our phone call. After a while, Reena and I headed towards the nearby doctor's clinic.

As Reena's head rested on my shoulder, I could feel that she was contemplating about something while tears streamed down her eyes relentlessly. I tried hard to decipher the expressions in her incomprehensible eyes, the feelings of a woman in love or with the concept of it, which was yet to be revealed to me. Her expressions pointed towards the fact that she was longing for solace and peace which she kept on searching, as her random eye movements indicated. My eyes fell on her dark-green sari—stained with drops of blood—that was elegantly draped around her small stature; her back slightly bent forward perhaps with pain that had suddenly accumulated in her right hand which she supported and rested on her lap. I noticed one or two grey hair in midst of her black tresses that were neatly tied in a bun. Her soft, tender eyes exposed her as an emotional being with an unusual strength, who was ready to endure anything that came her way with a brave face.

I recalled the very first time we met in the lab. She was a bubbly, young lady, a junior staff member of the biotech lab. In midst of my busy routine with experiments and report writing, her smiling face always gave an air of freshness, a charm that could hardly be articulated in words.

One day as I was working in the R&D lab, I noticed that sulphuric acid, one of the major ingredients of my experiment had got over. I went to the chemistry lab to borrow the chemical for my experiment.

As I walked inside the lab, I heard a group of junior female staff chatting amongst themselves in low, subdued voices. They continued with their conversation as I moved towards the area where they sat, oblivious to my presence.

'Reena has no shame.' One of them remarked, while the others nodded in agreement, taking pleasure in their judgemental remark.

'She has forgotten her dead husband so soon. It has not even been a year and she is going around with another guy.'

'A married guy.' Someone emphasized.

'She is a home-breaker.' The collective voices rattled the environment like a hailstorm hitting the window panes with its usual harshness.

I stood there like a dormant being, completely immovable. I felt like remonstrating with them over the damage that they were causing to Reena's reputation.

It was really shocking for me as all that I knew about Reena was her sweet smile and her happy-go-lucky attitude. I didn't imagine that her life could be as complicated as was the topic of discussion.

The group suddenly noticed me in the chemical lab and one of them asked—'Oh, ma'am! When did you come? Are you looking for something?'

'Yes. I need sulphuric acid for my experiment.' I said hesitantly, pondering on whether their conversation was part of a harmless, idle gossip or was there some truth in it. Or, was it an attempt to spread malicious rumour about Reena who was perhaps targeted by her jealous colleagues in a bid to defame her and take away the precious smile from her face, robbing her of her peace and content.

'Sure.' Vinita, a junior lab assistant, got up and moved towards the rack full of amber-coloured bottles.

'I know so little about my colleagues,' I wondered as I took the sulphuric acid bottle from Vinita, still trying to figure out the truth in their words.

Back in my lab, I could barely concentrate on my experiment. I was confused whether it was the monotony of the experiment or the story of Reena's personal life which disturbed me more. Anita, my colleague and boss, observed the uneasiness and asked about the issue that was bothering me. I narrated what I had heard from my colleagues in the other lab.

'People do talk about others. Don't they?' She said smilingly, patting my back in a friendly manner and in a soft voice, contrary to her hectoring tone. 'They do call you and me snob scientists.' She continued.

'But...' I felt disgusted and irritated—unable to come to terms with the reality that perhaps existed and I wasn't ready to see it the way others wanted me to perceive it.

'Oh! Come on. They'll say something or the other if they have nothing to do.' Anita moved to her workstation and settled down in her chair, avoiding the series of questions that she had anticipated I would pose to her.

I realized that she didn't wish to continue any further discussion on this topic. I tried to find out from her outward expressions how much she knew about Reena, whether she had the same opinion about her and had also been one of the gossip-mongers who had escaped my attention.

'We always see one side of the story.' She said, extending her vision to the glass panes of the window and beyond it, as if trying to see something that was concealed to the naked eye and was ready to be discovered by this young scientist. 'There could be more than what we can see.' She said after a meditative pause, her eyes moist with a strange emotion.

For the next few days, Reena didn't come to the lab. I met Vinita at the corridor on one of those days and enquired about the reason behind Reena's absence.

'We are not interested to know about her.' Vinita retorted, with some degree of condescension in her voice.

'But... Why?' I protested mildly, unable to fathom the reason behind her insensitive remark.

'A woman without values, a woman who has no respect for her dead husband ought to be ignored...' Vinita said a little breathlessly as if she was in a hurry to rush back to her work, and indulging in a conversation with me, and that too about Reena, was a sheer waste of time for her.

But her husband was no more and I wondered how and in what way she could exhibit her love and respect for him that could be visible to others.

'Perhaps you need to know her a little more.' I persisted vaguely, observing intently the doors of the chemistry lab that were behind Vinita, just to avert my eyes from her. She could sense the flicker of irritation that accompanied my words.

Vinita kept on staring at me, sizing me up, which I observed from the edge of my eyes. It could be that she wondered why I supported someone who seemed to be a wrongdoer in the eyes of the society, who should be made to suffer and not be pardoned until she expressed suitable penitence for what she had done.

I recalled that someone had told me once that Vinita had an abusive husband and was often found crying over the body marks that her treacherous husband gifted her in return of her love and respect for him. She never retaliated, chose to remain silent, or lacked the courage to protest, to raise a voice against the brutality that was loaded on her by her husband who got all the support of the indifferent society.

I looked at her straight in the eye and read the unsaid lines, 'You should have got attuned to societal expectations by now and should be following the norms like a civilized being.'

I'd always been ignorant of the weird rules and customs of society and its heightened expectations and perhaps never accepted them with grace and obedience that were prevalent in my counterparts.

'She is a bad example. Please don't ask any further.' Vinita said without a slightest note of embarrassment or discomfort in her tone, still clinging on to her societal values.

That was the last time I spoke to anybody about Reena, gradually learning to accept their mindset and also, that it would be impossible to change their outlook, the way they all perceived only one side of Reena's story. I, on the contrary, was destined to find more about her perspective and her way of looking at her own life through my brief understanding and knowledge about our existential issues that I'd gained on this planet.

A few days later, Reena returned to work.

'How are you?' I asked when we met in our R&D lab.

'I'm fine. My son was not well. He had malaria.' She said, showing her teeth in a voluptuous little smile.

'It must have been hard for you to manage everything on your own.' I said knowing that she stayed all by herself with her 5-year-old son.

It had been around 7–8 years that she'd been living in the small town Durgkunj, located in the southern Deccan Plateau region of India. The biotechnology lab brought her husband to this place where he worked as a senior scientist. Almost a year ago, he was diagnosed with cirrhosis of the liver, and as they said, he never responded to the medical treatment.

I closed my eyes imagining how hard it must have been for this young lady, singlehandedly managing her ailing husband on one hand and taking care of her son on the other. Those who had faced only knew about the torture and turmoil one had to undergo on seeing a loved one dying in front of one's own eyes. It must have been so dreadful to bear the traumatic experiences without any shoulder to cry on, without the support of any family member or a friend. It felt as if I could hear her heart-rending sobs, experience her deep sorrow that she had successfully hid beneath an outward calm and exhibition of content—a cloak of bejewelled smile, high spirits and congenial behaviour which seemed to be unreal for a moment.

'I could manage everything only because our doctor was beside us.' She said suddenly interrupting my thoughts. I noticed that I had been running my pen in circles around a figure in my notebook which suddenly became prominent on being encircled several times.

'Your family physician?' I couldn't control my curiosity, and put the pen down. 'Yes, Dr. Kunal. My husband's friend as well.' She returned with a smile, while settling down in a chair and motivating me to have a long conversation with her.

'Nice to hear that.'

'He's such a great man. He spent hours at our place giving all the mental support we needed.' Her eyes sparkled brightly, as if thousands stars had lit up at the same time.

'Oh!' I was unable to continue with the conversation, as I was constantly reminded of the gossip that I'd overheard in the chemistry lab about her—my mind constantly measuring the truth in every word she spoke and also, calculating my appropriate reaction that needed to be expressed on that basis.

'He wouldn't leave us alone. He always says that I give him a lot of happiness.' Reena was almost lost in her world, narrating how nice she felt on receiving the support of her dear friend who was a doctor. I observed a feeling of infatuation, a sense of love for this friend, which could hardly be explained in clear terms, as my knowledge seemed to be limited in that field of life.

'I'm sure you do.' I tried to maintain the mood of happiness that she had created with her lively hand movements and jovial narration.

'I have given him a reason to smile, a reason to be happy.' She said in a moment of exultation, giving me a strange, awkward feeling of not knowing how to react to her ecstasy and be happy with her.

'A good friend is meant to be so.' I somehow managed to utter these words. I was shy and inarticulate by nature, but always admired the innate ability in others to communicate the feelings of joy and discontent. In this case, I wanted the conversation to end as soon as possible as I felt like an intruder trespassing into her private life, even if she was willing to open the door of information about her personal affairs.

'You must be getting late for something. I'll come later.' Reena said sensing the uneasiness and impatience in me.

She left me in my lab wondering whether the doctor whom she claimed as her friend was the same person she had started seeing a few months after her husband's death.

Reena moved her head away from my shoulders, as I observed a strange anxiety in her eyes. Her right hand, with dark-red patches of blood clots all over, seemed to be tensed and numb from the blood loss, fatigued from the support of her left hand. Her left hand was positioned in a manner that it didn't hurt the delicate and injured portion any further, and perhaps this wearied her mind more than the muscles of both the hands, which stiffened and stretched taut across the shoulder blades and bones of her hands.

'Are you OK?' I asked, sounding as if we were going out for shopping and not to a doctor's clinic to control the damage that had occurred from the accident.

She pretended not to hear—disgusted with my enquiry after every minute or so.

After a while, she turned towards me, and said in a low voice with a grave expression, 'I'm fine.'

'Everything will be alright.' I said and tried hard to squeeze in a smile that must have appeared as a weak, unconvincing half-smile, which spontaneously got reflected in her irritated expression which said, 'How do you know? Are you a doctor?'

I felt embarrassed at my failed attempt to enliven her mood and to pretend that everything was fine or was going to be fine.

A bump on the road broke into our thoughts, and Reena let out a shriek.

'Be careful and drive slowly,' I blurted out loudly, in a bid to control the speed of the careless driver.

The ambulance didn't seem to have shock absorbers as our body tilted again and again from side to side whenever we encountered road bumps and potholes.

Reena averted her eyes from me and looked outside the window, her eyes still in a restless mode. I wondered what could have gone wrong, what was the cause behind her absentmindedness in the lab. She seemed to be disturbed about something for the past few days which was evident in the half-hearted smile that she gave me when we met occasionally. Was she feeling guilty about something? Was something bothering her? Was she afraid of the journey of love that she had undertaken?

'I'll die very soon.' She said incoherently. 'I miss him so much. I'll meet him only after death.' She continued in an almost inaudible voice, which was barely intelligible.

I preferred not to interrupt her brief soliloquy. At times we had to have such internal dialogues to relieve ourselves of the pain and sufferings.

I recalled a story about the Greek mythological character Orpheus who was known as the most-talented music player of the ancient times. He had a divinely gifted voice that could charm everyone who heard it. The myth said that no god or mortal could resist his music and even the rocks, trees would get moved by his music. Such was the power of love—it could move anybody and create a feeling in even the toughest of individuals.

Eurydice, a beautiful wood nymph, was enamoured by his voice. Eurydice and Orpheus soon felt the inexplicable bond of love between them. They decided to get married. But fate had planned something else for them. On the wedding night, Eurydice died of a snake bite.

Orpheus, bereaved of his beloved, decided to go to the underworld, the world of the dead, and get his wife back to the upperworld, the world of the living. It was a long, gruelling journey, during which he enchanted all including Hades, the God of the underworld, with his soft, mellifluous voice. Ultimately Hades promised that Eurydice would follow Orpheus to the world of the living. There was one condition that Orpheus would not look back till he and his wife had reached the upperworld for that would be the end of their journey and Eurydice would return to the underworld forever.

Perhaps that was the condition of love, a demand that one would not lose faith in the other no matter what the hardships were. Reena seemed to be losing faith in her newly-found love. Was she missing her dead husband? Or, torn between the love for her husband and Dr. Kunal? Was it possible for someone to love two people with the same passion and intensity?

The ambulance came to a screeching halt in front of a doctor's clinic. The driver opened the door for us. I helped Reena to get down from the ambulance and we proceeded towards the clinic.

There was nobody at the reception at that hour or perhaps the person was yet to come in. A man in white apron, with stethoscope coiled around his neck like a snake, came out of the other room.

'What's the matter? What happened?' His voice was heavy with concern.

'My colleague is bleeding profusely. Please attend her.' I said without any formal introduction.

'Sure. I'll examine her.'

He took her to the other room. As I proceeded along with them, he motioned for me to remain seated in the reception area. I turned towards Reena to assure her that everything would be alright, but was surprised to find a smile on her face—a sudden change which was unexpected. The person who was thinking about death all the while in the ambulance was suddenly happy and content. I always felt a strange kind of stomach ache, a numbness whenever I had to visit the doctor and that wouldn't go till I heard the magical words 'everything is alright; you'll get well very soon'. And over here she was relaxed and cheerful even before the doctor attended her.

After sometime, the doctor came out holding an X-ray film in his hand.

'The X-ray plate says that she has broken the distal phalanx. I mean the top-most bone of the index finger of her right hand.' He said with an air of seriousness lifting the X-ray film towards the light to show me the exact point of injury. I was too scared to even look at it.

'Does she know that?' I asked, toying with my mobile.

'No, I didn't tell her. Not sure whether she will be able to use her index finger anymore.' He explained as he sat down on the nearby table, dangling his legs in a rhythmic manner to the tune of his words.

'It's really unfortunate.' I said, imagining that it might not affect a doctor like him who had to deal with serious cases every single day of his life and couldn't afford to be emotional or even listen to such helpless grievances against fate.

'How did this happen?' He asked, taking interest in his patient and fixing his eyes on me.

'Even I am not sure.' I said, wondering that a brief spell of doubt about her love, a kind of agitation, a desire to be acknowledged by the world could be responsible for the accident.

Orpheus had also suffered for his disobedience, his loss of faith, his restlessness. When he started his journey out of the underworld with his wife, he was joyful that he would once again be reunited with his love. But on reaching the exit of the underworld, he was overpowered by a strong desire to see his beloved, feel her physical presence. The moment he stepped on the world of the living, he turned his head to hug his wife. Unfortunately, he got only a glimpse of Eurydice before she was once again drawn back into the underworld. He rushed back to the underworld again, but this time, he was denied entry and he lost his wife forever. A brief spell of doubt, a desire to feel the presence of his love in a physical form ruined his opportunity to have his beloved in his world. For a moment, his mind drifted into the physicality of the feeling of love that was always spiritual and divine and perhaps could not be perceived by the five senses alone. Love had to be felt with one's heart and soul, and a moment of one's own deception of its physical existence could take away its very presence, leaving the souls craving for love empty-handed and grieving forever.

I went inside and found Reena lying down on a bed and an X-ray machine was placed nearby.

'Dr Kunal has dressed my finger.' She said on seeing me. I was pleased and at the same time perplexed to find the same-old smile—which was lost for sometime—appear on her face which had shrivelled up from the trauma of the accident.

I searched for the lost faith, the content, the patience in her eyes—not sure whether I could find them, as I was lost for the first time in my life facing the unanswered questions that struggled within me, demanding a rational answer.

'Yes. I can see that.' I reciprocated her smile, relieved that I didn't have to pretend to console once again and say something that was never bound to come true.

'What went wrong?' Dr Kunal asked Reena, putting a hand on her shoulder.

She looked into his eyes like an obedient patient and responded to him with the usual eagerness to indulge in a long conversation that I had found in her on earlier occasions.

'I was preparing a mixture of *Jatropha* fruits. As the fruits were hard, they blocked the blade of the mixer. I tried to remove the hard fruits using my index finger without turning off the mixer. The blades were released suddenly and the accident happened.'

I observed a faint depression in her eyes when she narrated the incident to the doctor, which vanished within a fraction of a second.

'One can't be unmindful in a chemistry lab.' I said aloud, feeling sorry that my presence in the lab couldn't avoid an accident of that sort.

'I'll take care of her and also, drop her home.' Dr Kunal told me all of a sudden.

'Get well soon.' I kissed Reena on the forehead and hugged her warmly, without knowing that we were saying good-bye to each other for the very last time, as she wasn't going to return to the lab.

'I won't allow her to work in the lab anymore.' Dr Kunal said as he walked me till the door of his clinic.

'Ah! Yes, she should take up some other work.' I said thoughtfully.

'Don't worry. I'll look after her.' He said, observing my worried expressions.

I looked into his eyes and said, 'I know you will take good care of her. Let her not have any doubt in her mind.'

'I'll see to that.'

I got on the ambulance. I looked out the window of the ambulance and noticed Dr Kunal waiving at me—a genuine feeling of love, overwhelming his face and body.

That day I realised that love was always pure, immortal—seldom depended on the material gain, real-life situations and practical outlook of society. A surge of doubt could momentarily affect the physical beings who were in love but all of that lasted for a short while till they united spiritually in their own world.

Souporno Mukherjee

Souporno, 17, is a higher secondary pass out student with science from Pitts Modern School, Gomia. He resides in India, the country he loves to the core, in a place named Bokaro Thermal in the state of Jharkhand. He is passionate about writing and also has keen interest in football. He likes watching and playing the sport and supporting his favorite football club, FC Barcelona. He also likes watching movies and listing music.

You can reach him at – <u>writinsam@gmail.com</u>

8

A WALLET, A BRIEFCASE AND THE RAIN

Souporno Mukherjee

"The rain began again. It fell heavily, easily, with no meaning or intention but the fulfillment of its own nature, which was to fall and fall." - Helen Garner

MUMBAI
25th July, 2005

The dim yellow lights of the *dhaba* and the dark sky were the color shades that night. Prashant, a young man in his mid-twenties, in his long full sleeved oversized shirt, a clean shaven face and long hair sat on one of the benches, holding his head. Lost in his deepest thoughts under the yellow light bulb, he lit a cigarette. A thin boy of about ten years of age, placed a steaming cup of tea before him. Prashant looked at the glass cup and then at the light bulb above him, smoking his cigarette. He then picked up the cup and took a sip, it burned his tongue and he immediately placed the cup on the table and held his tongue out.

"Give it some time, the tea will cool down."

A man in his early sixties sat before him smiling with a cup of tea in his hand. Prashant could see his wrinkled oily face, his hair and his broad smile. He tried to smile back keeping his thoughts aside.

"Looks like the burn has made it difficult to even smile." The man spoke again, taking a sip from his cup.

This time Prashant smiled naturally.

"You look charming with that smile." The old man winked.

"Life doesn't allow you to smile every day." Prashant spoke for the first time.

The old man smiled again and placed his empty cup on the table.

"Myself, Mukesh Deshpande." The old man extended his hand.

"Prashant Kulkarni." Prashant said switching his half burnt cigarette to his left hand and extending the other one.

"So, here is Mr. Prashant, a young fellow with a cigarette in his hand and hot steaming tea before him. You can tell me how a cup of tea is troubling you." Mukesh continued smiling and signaled the *dhaba* boy to bring him another cup of tea.

"It's not the tea, it is life." Replied Prashant smoking his cigarette.

"What's the difference?" asked Mukesh wittily.

"Tea burns just the skin, while life burns something inside you. Something you cannot touch but only feel, something which has no medicine, no cure." Prashant took a sip from his cup, this time it was fine though.

"You can tell me." Mukesh replied, as the boy placed another cup of tea before him.

The light flickered once or twice, Prashant looked up and sighed.

"This world runs on paper. Money. My aunt is ill and her condition is worsening by the day. I need some pieces of paper. I need money." Prashant tried sipping his tea again but it had turned too cold by then, he spat back the contents in the glass.

"Neither too hot, nor too cold. Tea tastes best somewhere between the two." Mukesh sipped from his cup.

Prashant stared at his cup, his eyes almost watery.

"I wish I could help." Mukesh said playing with the gold ring he had worn in his ring finger. "I mean with the money."

Prashant was still looking at the glass. Mukesh had a look at his watch.

"I guess it's time to leave." Mukesh said placing his hand over Prashant's. He noticed the ring in Mukesh's finger shining bluntly under the flickering dim light.

A thought crossed his mind and Prashant kept looking intently at the ring. Suddenly the light flickered violently and Prashant got up from his seat and inched towards the *dhaba* owner.

"Eight rupees Mukesh Bhai and four yours." The *dhaba* owner said raising his head from an old notebook.

Mukesh slid his hand inside the right pocket of his trouser and then the left and then he searched violently every pocket that his clothes had to offer. His face turned white and he ran back to the bench where he had been sitting.

"I think I dropped my wallet somewhere." Mukesh said, pale faced. Again searching his pockets.

Prashant kept looking blankly and from his shirt pocket he took out a ten rupee note and one five rupee coin and handed it to the *dhaba* owner. The dhaba owner returned him three one rupee coins. Prashant slid them back in his shirt pocket, lit up another cigarette and left.

"I shall pay you later, keep it noted." Mukesh still had a hand in his pocket, hoping to find the wallet.

The *dhaba* owner returned a half smile. "Your friend paid for it already."

Prashant was staring at the overcast sky through the window beside his bed. The dark patches had left no blue, like a little boy's painting gone wrong. Drowsiness had started captivating Prashant after a restless night. Laying on his back he closed his eyes for some moments. Nevertheless he had to reopen them again, the ceiling fan kept moving above him. The dark patches on the roof might have become even darker now, but he had never seen them darkening. It was like a sudden realization to him. Prashant turned his eyes to his aunt, she let out a low moan lying under an old rag, and her head turned in the opposite direction. Prashant looked at her for a sometime, he noticed the wrinkles on her neck and patches of grey on her head. Her bangles made some jingling sound when she moved her hand a bit. He remembered her working in the mill, her bangles jingling more cheerfully than they were today. He remembered the smile on her face when she turned back and saw Prashant standing beside him. Those smiles could rarely be seen now, but Prashant hadn't noticed just like he had overlooked the back patches on the roof. The roof under which he slept night after night.

His eyes now shifted to the brown leather wallet in his hand. The sides of the wallet had worn out probably due to prolonged usage. Prashant opened the wallet and it spread into two halves. The left half had a small transparent pocket and there was a small grainy picture of a woman. The woman in the picture was wearing a green colored *sari* and the most pleasant smile Prashant had ever seen. She might have lined her eyes with kohl but it was not clear though, her hair had been left loose, her lips were painted pink and her cheeks fluffy. Prashant kept staring at the picture, he then pulled it out from the pocket and had a close look at it. A low moan again and Prashant quickly replaced the picture in the pocket and hid the wallet under his pillow as he saw his aunt turn around and signal for something. The jingles were heard again.

Prashant went up to her and placed his ear near her lips. All he could make out was '*wata...wata*'.

He fetched an old aluminum glass and filled it with water from a bucket, went to his aunt and held the glass near her mouth. After she had had enough, he emptied the left over in the bucket again.

Empty bottles of vitamins and packets of medicines kept rolling on the table before him. He picked a packet and found only one surviving tablet in it. Sweat drops were now visible clearly on Prashant's forehead. He fetched another glass of water and emptied it in a gulp. Next he lifted his pillow, took out the wallet and sat near entrance of the little one room shelter where he had lived all his life. The room had just one window to let some air flow in, there were two folding beds which were now almost a decade old on either side of the two walls facing each other. On one of them hung an old picture of lord Krishna, standing with a flute in his hand. Some utensils were left at one corner of the sparsely lit room and the other corner had a wooden table loaded with medicines and a water bucket near its foot. The walls had black patches all over them, red mud bricks could be seen at places where the plaster had worn off.

Prashant reopened the wallet, he took out the picture again had another look. This time he could see some more details. The fair fluffy cheeks, the long brows and a pendant around her neck. There was something in that old grainy picture that compelled Prashant to keep looking at it. He replaced the picture in the pocket again this time more carefully though. The wallet had two hundred rupee notes, four ten rupee notes, a five hundred rupee note and some coins in a little pocket. He also found a bill and two cards in it. One of them had Mukesh's picture in it along with his name and address printed on it, it was his driving license another was a visiting card, it also had Mukesh's name printed on it along with his office address and cell phone number. After inspecting the wallet thoroughly, the closed it for the second time that morning and placed it in his shirt pocket.

Prashant kept sitting at the doorstep looking up towards the sky which was darkening with time, like his aunt health. Two crows flew over him. Somewhere far, someone was hitting a metallic object constantly, two dark faced women carrying water pots passed nearby. The whole of Dharavi seemed to slow down before his eyes, as the clock paced. Stealing was never in his blood but there was nothing that he could do, he had reached the dead end. Some naked slum children brushed past him rolling a cycle tire as he got up to enter his shelter.

Inside, the fan was still running, the walls were still black, his aunt was still moaning and the room now looked even dark. Prashant knelt before his aunt and gave her the last surviving tablet. She somehow raised her head, took the medicine in her mouth and then swallowed minimal water with shaking hands.

"I feel...feel... restless." She somehow managed to say holding her chest with her left hand and handing the empty glass to Prashant with other.

Prashant wanted to say something but the words remained in his mouth and his eyes watered. He just helped her lay back.

Another look at the wallet and he had that five hundred rupee note in his hand. Prashant did not feel the guilt, he just swallowed the lump in his throat, put on his slippers and left. On his way he saw people lying on the street on old rags, children crying on the street, some young men smoking at a distance. The congested, crowded alleys of Dharavi suddenly seemed to broaden by inches. Prashant could hear nothing except his heartbeat. He lowered his head and kept walking until he could see the medical shop where he had been many a times to get medicines for his aunt.

The moment he raised his head he saw two things before him and stood there motionless. First, Gulmohar Medical Store printed in big bold letters. Second, Mukesh Deshpande with his trademark smile. The muted world around Prashant resumed and Prashant could do no more than stare blankly at Mukesh and his smile.

"So you got those pieces of paper." Mukesh's smile broadened.

Prashant could not meet his eyes. His heartbeat was now even faster and even louder. Did Mukesh know that he had stolen his wallet? Was he waiting here purposely? Would he beat him up? Prashant's mind kept shooting all sorts of negative thoughts. He somehow smiled a broken smile.

"Why is it that you always find it difficult to smile? What is it that is troubling you today? See, I lost my wallet and I am still smiling."

Prashant's nervousness was visible enough. His sweat drops now even bigger than they were when he had seen those empty medicine packets. He wiped his forehead with the sleeve of his shirt and went straight to the shopkeeper and handed the medical slip.

"Give me all of them, fast." He wiped his forehead again.

The shopkeeper had a look at the paper and went in to fetch the medicines. Prashant hesitantly had to turn his head towards Mukesh. He was still smiling, as if he knew everything.

In the backdrop Prashant saw a man in the adjacent shop along with a child. The boy kept pestering him for chocolates. Some people were busy buying ration from the nearby ration shop. Two boys cycled past them ringing their bells. At some distance some people were quarrelling for some reason. Prashant's gaze shifted back to the child, who was still begging for some chocolates.

"What...what are you doing here?" Prashant finally managed to speak, fumbling.

"Ah, it's this headache, came over to take some painkillers and to have a look at my shop." said Mukesh looking towards the hoarding of the medical store.

Prashant was tongue tied, he looked at the shop once then towards Mukesh.

Mukesh took out a wallet from his back pocket. Prashant could tell that it was new and the smell of leather was fresh.

"Got it this morning only." Mukesh said, showing the wallet. "I didn't lose much money but I lost my driving license and the only picture of my wife."

Prashant remembered the woman in the old grainy picture. Her necklace, her fluffy cheeks, her green colored sari, her pleasant smile. The boy was now leaving with chocolates in one hand, and the other holding his father's, smiling to himself.

Mukesh took out a card from his wallet and handed it to Prashant. Mukesh's name, his office address, his phone number. The same card that he had taken out from the wallet that morning. Although he had read it once, Prashant still kept re-reading the card.

"In case you need any help from me." Prashant heard Mukesh say, while he was still looking at the card.

Guilt was now conquering Prashant. He remembered his aunt, the old grainy picture, the driving license. His eyes were filled up to the brim.

"Sir, your medicines." The shopkeeper placed a packet before him.

Prashant somehow held back his tears and buried his hands in his pocket and took out the five hundred rupee note. As he was about to hand it to the shopkeeper, someone held him back. Mukesh, it was.

"No need, you can keep them." Mukesh handed him the packet. "You paid for my tea last night, can't I return you the favor?" He smiled.

"But…" Prashant had hardly managed to say a word when Mukesh held his hand and made him keep the note back in his pocket.

Prashant could do no more. He started sobbing, then he placed his hands over his eyes and started weeping placing the packet at the counter.

"My aunt is ill, please help me. She is the only one I have. My aunt is ill." He kept weeping.

Mukesh hugged him tight and tried to calm him down. But the tears won't stop like the heavy rain, he continued weeping.

"See, I gave you my card. It has my phone number, call me whenever you feel like, whenever you need any help. I don't mind spending pieces of paper if it can save one's life."

Mukesh's words were like those of a father's to Prashant. He calmed down and Mukesh kept patting his back.

"Everything will be alright." Mukesh added and again handed the packet to him.

The overcast sky kept getting dark with every passing second. It was as if the clouds were holding back their water as Prashant had held his, but they could burst any moment.

"Now run back home and give your aunt the medicines, it's going to rain any moment."

Mukesh's smile was back but now it was more of a reassuring smile. A smile which meant he was willing to help. A smile which meant that he would be standing beside Prashant whenever he needed. His smile told everything. Prashant thanked him and started walking homewards.

The sky grew darker with every step that Prashant took. He saw men, drenched in sweat running back home, women were picking up clothes they had left outside to dry, children being forced inside by their parents. Prashant had a look at the sky again and then he paced up, his cheeks still wet. Prashant's thoughts shifted from Mukesh to his aunt and then back to Mukesh again. Prashant remembered the *Dhaba*, he remembered how tensed Mukesh had been when he had lost his wallet. He wished he had not stolen, he wished he had just been friendly but then the bullet had already left the gun and there was no way that Prashant could bring it back. Prashant heard the clouds roar and he speeded up again.

Prashant had hardly reached his place when a small crowd caught his attention. He feared the worst and started running. A young fellow, dark complexioned wearing half pants came running towards Prashant.

"Your aunt is serious. We heard her moaning and went in. There she was on the floor, panting."

Prashant's face turned white, he rushed into the crowd and went to his aunt and held her hand.

"Don't worry aunty, you will be alright."

Someone from the crowd provided him with a cell phone. The first person that came to his mind was, Mukesh. The one he had robbed last night, the one who had helped him selflessly, the one who had hugged him when he needed. He took out the card from his pocket and dialed his number.

Sitting on the cold metal chair of the hospital Prashant rewound time in his mind, the hot tea, meeting Mukesh, picking his pocket, paying his bill, the picture of the woman, the medical store, Mukesh and his smiling face. Prashant, in his twenty six years of his life had never met such a selfless man before, who had helped him without demanding any return, who had at once sent his driver with a huge sum of money to escort his aunt to the hospital. His eyes were liquid, but the tears refused to roll down. How can a man be so generous? Just a night's conversation, a stolen wallet and now he was more than a family member to him. Lost in his thoughts Prashant looked out of a window nearby, it wasn't raining but he could tell that it would any moment.

An attendant tapped his shoulder.

"Your aunt is better now, you can meet her."

Standing outside the translucent glass door of the 'Intensive Care Unit' Prashant saw a hazy figure of his aunt. All wrapped in a white cloth only except her face, lifeless and still. He pushed the door open and walked in. He now saw that there were innumerous pipes around her which were not visible through the door. He sat on a stool beside the bed staring at his aunt's face. There was absolute silence, but there was no peace. Prashant saw the first few drops of rain on the window pane, silently dripping down and so was the water in his eyes. Life had been worse, but had worsened further from the moment he had picked up that wallet. 'Give it some time, the tea will cool down.' Mukesh had said. Prashant knew there was truth in what he had said, at least he thought so.

He held her wrinkled lifeless hand for some time and kept looking at her face now and then. She was breathing heavily, Prashant could tell by the rise and fall of her chest. At last he got up and turned to leave. A faint, weak voice stopped him from pushing the door open. He went back to his aunt, this time her eyes were half opened, she signaled Prashant to come closer. Prashant stooped over her and brought his ear close to her lips.

"Uhh...Beta...I think..urgh..my days are over." Saline water kept dripping down Prashant's eyes, he could say nothing, just listen.

"Will you..urgh..um do ...urgh..do a last...urgh...uhh...thing for me?"

Prashant pressed his lips and nodded.

"Ahh...then...then go back home...uhhh and..urgh...and bring me...my..urgh..my briefcase."

Prashant nodded again and turned to leave wiping his eyes with the sleeve of his shirt. He heard her say, "Under...urgh...under the bed.."

He saw her chest rise and fall rapidly as he left the room.

Hard, heavy drops of rain landed on Prashant's body as he left the hospital. He remembered the phone conversation with Mukesh. 'Please tell me everything is fine.' Mukesh said when he received the call. He had sent a servant with pieces of paper, money. 'I am sending you the money immediately and I will be there as soon as possible, your aunt will be fine.' The servant informed Prashant about Mukesh's headache which had worsened even after taking the medicines.

The rains thickened however they couldn't stop Prashant from walking his way back home. Fully drenched he finally pushed the door open. Aunty had asked to bring her briefcase, the one which she had kept only to her ever since Prashant had seen it. Many a times he had begged his aunt to open the briefcase but she never would and as time passed Prashant gave up and it shifted under her bed and remained untouched. Prashant tripped over a bowl and almost fell down. He sat down on the floor and looked around. The room was quite dark, there was no electricity. He could see the bowl shining from the little light that entered the room through the open door. He could now see his bed, his pillow, and the wallet that lay hidden beneath it. Prashant composed himself and crawled under his aunt's bed. Cobwebs and mosquitoes welcomed him, his head hit the bed once or twice and Prashant had to lower himself down further. His hand landed on a hard box shaped object and he pulled it out.

He sat near the door, the same place where he had earlier that morning. His aunt's bed was empty, her thin wrinkled body was missing. The house suddenly looked quite bigger or maybe it looked more vacant. Prashant dusted the cobwebs and dirt off the briefcase with his hand. Looking at its deep brown color and the golden lock on the top Prashant felt nostalgic. Many dust coated memories in his mind had now been dusted off. Prashant smiled wryly looking at the briefcase. He sat there in silence for some time, hearing the sound of the rain hitting the roof and looking at the briefcase. The cold air touched his wet body and he shivered. After some time he went back inside and joined his hands before the old picture of lord Krishna hanging near his aunt's bed. He closed his eyes and prayed for the first time in many months. Drops of water kept sliding down the corner of his eyes and he prayed in silence only the sound of the rain accompanying him.

With water dripping off his clothes Prashant re-entered the hospital; the briefcase held close to his chest. The bright lights were no more glowing now.

"There is shortage of power supply sir." The receptionist said looking up from a long register.

Prashant could wait no longer, he hurried past some nurses towards the intensive care unit. He wanted to see his aunt again, talk to her again and give her the briefcase. For some strange reason he was getting restless. Prashant pushed the glass door open and went in but there was silence. The hospital ward suddenly looked even bigger or maybe more vacant. The bed was empty.

Prashant remained still for few moments and then the door flung open again. A man in a long white coat and a notebook in his hand entered the room. Although Prashant wanted to say something the words remained inside him, teardrops reappeared instead.

"Your aunt's health deteriorated and we had to operate immediately. I hope she will be fine soon."

Prashant did not say a word, his eyes were the only ones to speak. He sat down on the floor and grabbed the briefcase close to him.

The sky kept darkening and the rains kept pouring continuously. Prashant was now sitting on the same metal chair where he had earlier. Thousand thoughts in his mind and one of them being Mukesh. 'I will be there as soon as possible.' He had said over the phone. Prashant looked out through the window at some distance, all he could see was water pouring from the skies. 'It must have been the weather that has kept him away.' he thought.

He picked up the briefcase and walked up to the window. A few drops of rain landed on his face. Prashant's clothes had dried up by then but the feeling of wetness returned with the landing of the water drops. He placed the briefcase on the window sill and looked out at nothingness. The buildings looked hazy behind the falling drops of rain, the water logged streets, the overflowing drains, the closed shops. From his shirt pocket Prashant took out a wet piece of paper, it had 'Mukesh Deshpande' printed on it along with his phone number. The card which Mukesh had given him earlier that morning. Prashant headed straight towards the reception.

"Excuse me, can I make a phone call?" Prashant pointed to the telephone at the reception.

"Sorry sir, but all telephone and mobile towers are down at the moment." came the reply.

Prashant looked at the card in his hand once and then silently pocketed it and went back to the chair. The restlessness inside him kept growing. He wanted to meet his aunt and give her the briefcase. He wanted to talk to Mukesh once but he could only sit and wait for the clock to tick.

The man in the white coat stood before Prashant.

"Her condition is getting critical but we are trying to give our best." He said putting one hand on Prashant's shoulder.

Prashant had all his life known only one person and it was only that one person he had in his family. Prashant's father had left when he had been just a month old and his mother died soon after. This was all Prashant knew, his aunt had told him on his sixteenth birthday. He had never really wanted to know about his parents because of the love that his aunt had given him was more than he could wish for. But that day sitting on the chair outside the hospital Prashant wished he had his mother by his side and his father helping him in every way he could. He felt like an orphan for the first time in his life.

Two more tries to call Mukesh but the telephone lines were still dead. More restlessness and even more anxiety. Prashant's eyes switched places around him, the rains, the ticking of the clock, the briefcase in his hand, the operation theatre, and the nurses. Every minute seemed to last an hour, as if time had stopped flowing for a while. Amidst the silence in Prashant's world there was a 'click' sound and the briefcase opened up.

'His aunt is smiling under her white covering, Prashant is handing the briefcase to her. She looks happy, takes it from him and blows him a kiss and he is contented with her smile.' Prashant had imagined the scene a thousand times over in his mind but there he was with the briefcase, open and its contents before him. With shaking hands he picked up the first piece of paper. It was a will in which his aunt had handed over all what she had to Prashant. There was a half knit hand woven sweater, a purse which had a picture of his aunt and some money in it and there was another folded piece of paper. Prashant took it out safely, someone had written something on it and the blue colour of the pen could be seen. The sides of the paper had turned yellow indicating its age. He unfolded the paper, a small photograph slid out and fell down on the floor. Prashant picked it up to see what he had never imagined. The same green colored sari, the pleasant smile, the loose hair, the pink lipstick, the long brows and the pendant around the neck. The same grainy picture he had found in Mukesh's purse. His heart started racing as Prashant started reading the letter.

"Dear Prashant,

I must have gone when you read this letter. The world has been a bitter place but seems worthwhile when I see your lovely little face. I always wanted to have a child like you and live rest of my life caring for you. Now that I have you I shall never let you go. You are just a year old now but soon you will grow up to be a big man and the day is not far away when I will have to answer you about your parents. Till date I was rather being selfish, please forgive me for that. I had decided to let you know the least about your parents so that I can keep all your love to me. Probably when you read this letter you might have tears in your eyes and you might even get angry at me but please forgive me for keeping this away from you for so long.

Your mother was left alone when your father decided to pack the bag one day and walk away for some reason I still don't know. Maybe he had found more love in someone or something else. I could have walked around the city to find him but as I said earlier I wanted to have all your love, I am sorry again. Soon after your mother died and on her death bed she handed you over to me. The rest of the story is all what you know now. There is something more that I want you to know. If you find a half knitted sweater along with this letter keep it because it is priceless as it was made by your mother. I am also keeping the only photograph of you mother along with this letter. I wanted to give it to you earlier but again forgive me for that too.

This was all what I had to say. I wish you a long and happy life ahead. My love and blessings shall always be with you.

Your Selfish Aunt,
Meera."

There was a loud thundering outside and Prashant burst into more tears so did the sky. A drop or two landed on the letter in his hand. He picked up the sweater and grabbed it tightly. The wool had been touched by his mother, the sweater had been knitted by her. He looked at the grainy photograph again and caressed it lovingly. Then he cried some more and felt the letters inscribed on the paper.

Prashant felt someone's presence before him. A man in white coat stood there with his head hung low and before he could say anything Prashant heard him say.

"I am sorry Mr. Kulkarni we couldn't save her."

Night had fallen in but the rains continued. Voices echoed inside the hospital and Prashant stood near a window watching the downpour. 'I didn't lose much money but I lost my driving license and the only picture of my wife.' he remembered Mukesh's words. Mukesh was his father and Prashant had been a thief to him. Looking at the dark red sky Prashant remembered the grainy picture that he had seen so closely that morning. His aunt had left him but with something that he had to carry for the rest of his life. He wanted to go to Mukesh and hug him again and cry on his father's shoulder. He waited and waited and it continued to rain.

It must have been about eight thirty the following morning when the rains ceased and Prashant left the hospital with his aunt's body to the funeral. He wanted to meet his dad and wanted him to be there with him but this time he wanted to be a new Prashant before him, one who was not a thief but one who was his long lost son. He walked back home once again through the water logged streets of Dharavi. Children were crying, women were weeping, houses had fallen down and there was misery all around. Prashant remembered his walk to home the previous day, everything had been so quiet and only the rain kept pouring, his aunt was alive then, the briefcase had not been opened and he didn't know that Mukesh was his father.

As Prashant entered his place for the first time that morning he found water inside his house. The roof had fallen down and washed away all that lay around. Only the two beds and the old picture of lord Krishna were in place. Prashant found his pillow drenched in water and the wallet underneath had also soaked water. He picked it up and wiped it with the sleeve of his shirt. He then took out a wet crumpled five hundred rupee note from his pocket and placed it in the wallet.

Prashant now had only one thought in his mind and that was Mukesh and he was his only hope, the only one he could now call family. He walked to the medical shop where he had met him the last time, the shop was half open and two men were smoking inside.

Prashant peeped in, "Excuse me may I know where the owner of this shop Mukesh Deshpande lives?"

The two of them exchanged glances then one of them took out a paper, jotted down the address and handed it to Prashant.

Before the two storied building stood Prashant. There was a huge iron gate with rods painted in black and just beside it on the wall on a piece of marble 'Deshpande Villa' had been engraved. Prashant knew now that his surname had been Deshpande. Prashant opened the gate and walked in.

He stood there in the little garden outside the house watching the dead marigold plants and the muddy patches. Someone tapped his shoulder. It was the same man who had come to deliver the money for his aunt's treatment.

"How can I help you?"

"I came here to meet Mukesh Deshpande."

"But he can't meet anyone right now."

Prashant looked at the man, his dark sunburned face and the sweat dripping off his head.

"Why?" he asked almost silently.

"He had a severe headache but we couldn't reach the hospital on time due to the heavy rains. The headache worsened further and he got paralyzed last night. The doctors say he can neither move or talk but can only see and listen people now." The man looked towards the window right to the door.

Between the gaps of the curtains Prashant saw Mukesh lying on a bed. There were two women around him and he kept looking blankly at everyone. For a second his eyes turned towards Prashant but Prashant looked away.

"I am..so..sorry." His voice choked and again his eyes spoke for him. He took out the wallet from his pocket and handed it to the man.

Prashant left the Deshpande Villa to never return again. In his mind he had this scene repeating itself over and over again –

Mukesh is smiling and Prashant is giving him his wallet saying that the Dhaba owner found it the other day. Mukesh is thanking him and asking for a cup of tea. Prashant smiling and replying, 'I am your son.' A scene which never came true! Yes, life is ironic!

Meghna Gupta Jogani

- Meghna Gupta Jogani has Masters (M.A.) in English Major from Shreemati Nathibai Damodar Thackersey Women's University, Mumbai (2000). "Once a student of Literature, always a Literature student" is her belief. She has taken to writing, with a view to contributing to society at large and bring about a change in perspectives for the better. Almost all her writings, poems and short stories, have a social issue at their core, aiming for the reader to grasp and appreciate. She has authored "Padchinh" (2012), a collection of her poems in Hindi, portraying a woman's life journey in five stages, dedicated to women. The book was launched on 15 August, 2012 at The Little Theatre, NCPA, Mumbai, by renowned gynaecologist Dr. Kusum Zaveri.

- She won the 3rd position in the prestigious "3rd Rabindranath Tagore International English Poetry Competition", 2014, organised by PoisiesOnline in Odisha, 2014 for her poem "Superwoman".

- In the "National Poets' Meet" held during the same event, she won 1st position in two categories: "Poetry Recitation" for her poem "Masterpiece" and "Poetry Writing" (topic and title both given).

- She has her work published vis a vis contributing them to reputed Publications in following order:

- "Where's my Sunday?", poem published in "Anthesis" Anthology, 2014, by Xpress Publications.

- An Epitaph published in "Epitaphs" Anthology, 2014, by InnerChildPress and Shambhabi Publications in collaboration.

- "1...2...3...Fight!" A short story published in "Minds@ Work 3", 2014, Anthology of Short Stories by FirstStep Pavingsway Press.
- "Universe Within Me" poem published in WOW (World Of Words) online magazine.
- "Every Man" a poem and few more works like "Joyride of a Lifetime" a short love story and "Don't color me Black and Red" a short story on Holi, few poems in Hindi for Republic Day etc. published on "WriteConnect India" online portal.
- "Say it with orchids" short story published by Partridge (Penguin) in "Catalogue of Memories" Anthology of Short Stories (ongoing).
- "Born @ 35" short story published by Airavat Publishers in "Mighty Thoughts" Anthology of Short Stories.
- "Let's start all over again" poem published in "Heavenly Hymns" 2015, Anthology by Xpress Publication.
- "One Sun, One Moon" poem in "Muse For World Peace" Anthology of Contemporary Poets, 2015.
- "Let our Hearts Make Love Tonite" poem in "Just For You, My Love" Anthology of love poems by The Poetry Society of India, 2015.
- "Mark Of Her Lipstick on His Collar" a short story to be published by Numerique Publications in "31 Crimes" Anthology.
- few more submissions await confirmations.
- An anthology of love poems, co-authored, is soon on the cards for release by December 2015 too.
- She is an active speaker in several groups as well where she has recited her poems :
1. Indian Cultural Centre, Bangkok. (ICC)
2. Thailand Hindi Parishad, Bangkok.

3. Indian Embassy, Bangkok.
4. HIVE, Mumbai.
- Her poems have been published in some newspapers as well:
- "कोख की चीख" and "मैं एक औरत हूँ" in separate issues of नवभारत अवकाश dated 17 June, 2012 and 2012 respectively.
- "फिर से सरफ़रोशी की तमन्ना" in साहित्य दर्पण dated 16 October 2013.
- She has now taken to writing novels. Several of her manuscripts are in the near completion stage. She wishes to publish
  "The Blushing Maiden ", a Romantic fiction saga,
  set in Rajasthan, as her debut Novel next.

9

"SAY IT WITH ORCHIDS"

Meghna Gupta Jogani

A bespectacled, sober Gujarati boy, a happy-go-lucky, naive Punjabi girl, the honey-sweet fragrance of orchids and a few mouth-watering "milk sweets" from "the best dairy farm", are all that make up this yet another love story! Simple ingredients you'd think, but a not-so-simple recipe...

It took a somewhat long and complicated "preparation time", before it could be served "piping hot" to you, my dear readers. Let's give you the whole background and take a learning class till you dig it.

His glasses had nearly slipped down his nose and fallen off his face, when he had seen her, being shown the way to the cabin, just adjacent to his own. His Secretary, Mrs. Patra, had come in shortly, with a bunch of beautiful orchids smiling from her hand, walking up to the table darting them one by one into the empty vase.

"Good Morning Sir! The new Manager, has just joined in from today, and has been handed over all pending assignments. Her name is Mrs. Dhingra. There... Have a good day Sir!" she spoke jovially while arranging things around in the "Boss' Cabin". She had been given standing orders to invariably bring orchids - every morning, a different color though. He nodded in approval, and smiled granting permission for her to leave.

After she left, he looked at the orchids; a long, magnetized look, feeling awesome about them, like always, but today was something, even more special. The hypnotic fragrance of the flowers, had started working its magic on him, and had pulled him towards them, and then slowly into his own past...

The freedom-loving and fearless sunshine of the princely, coastal port-town of Porbandar, made its way, trudging through the pigeons, perched cuddling to each other, on the window-sill, while watching Jaison sleeping peacefully, and gently warmed his facial skin.

He got up, almost immediately, cheerful as usual, and greeted his avian friends, before they took off. An energetic, jolly boy, had now grown up into a sober, young adult. His family was so very proud of him! The only one in the whole neighbourhood (read town), to have been selected, for the admissions to the prestigious ABC College of Engineering, Bangalore. Bangalore! How he had spent sleepless nights trying to figure out the life of a bustling city in his dreams...

He had studied endless nights, competing with the stars; it seemed, to stay awake. No financial extravaganzas showered on him, from his modest middle-class family of coconut harvesters- how he aspired to work towards the betterment of his lot! He had toiled willingly in the afternoon sun, helping on the farms of his father and uncles, studied the nights away, through to college. His efforts had finally paid off, with the confirmation letter flying like a kite in hand, when he had broken the news to his family members, and would now serve as the rocket to transport him to a new world!

The normally jovial household, hustling and bustling with innumerable activities, was silent this morning. All the members, had gone to Kirti Temple, as was their ritualistic practise, before the commencement of any auspicious occasion, like birth, marriage, inaugurations, (and now admission to a city college), and get blessings and inspiration for the "rightful path" of living. At the station, he took leave of his friends and cousins, who looked up to him as an example to follow, his uncles and aunts, all of whom loved him as their own child, the loving reminders, that sounded more like reprimands, of his mother, to take care of himself, his father's concern to not fall into bad company...he took leave from all.

He left them standing behind, diminishing in size as the train carried him forwards to his future. He took a short nap, only to be rudely and abruptly disturbed by the ruckus of vendors, and travellers in a frenzy to catch seats and get settled. He had to change train at Rajkot Junction, he was feeling restless- he just couldn't afford to miss it. A heart-racing and a head-pounding journey later, he was finally headed to college!

He took in eyefulls of the city sights, the amazement, the delight, the awe ... Even more magnificent than his dreams! "Yes Sir," he answered to the Matron of Boys' Hostel, when asked if he ate vegetarian meals. He was lead up a creaking old stairway to the third floor. He had another roommate, a Tamil boy named Parimal, (as shy as he was dark) - he had blushed slightly when Jaison had entered. Drained from the journey, he had slept like a log.

The next morning, he diligently got ready and wore the new, cream shirt his mother had so lovingly sewed. He explored the environment eagerly. How different from home! As he seated himself in class, he noticed a bit uncomfortably, how the boys and girls sat next to each other freely. His observations were suddenly called off by a chorus of giggles!

He turned around to see what it was all about, when his attention got focussed on her...the poor girl had stumbled over her own dupatta, and was fumbling herself clumsily up. "Welcome Ms. Peacock," someone chimed; her dress was a riot of colors. He was stunned by their rudeness and apathy, and instead got up himself to give her a hand. "Thank you ji," she said sweetly while hesitantly clasping around it.

After the chaos subsided and the lecturer marched in, he eyed her from the corners of his eyes. She was absent-mindedly adjusting her dress as though undecided which way she preferred it. The query that arose in his mind, was answered when the lecturer called "Lovleen Chadha!" on the attendance register, and she had replied, "Haan ji, present!" After class, much to his own surprise, his heartbeat repeated "Lovleen...Lovleen..." in rhythm. He even imagined her in a traditional "chaniya-choli", sitting on his garden swing outside their house, swinging, and who should be standing behind her, pushing her to gleeful heights...!

He had not expected this to happen. Here he was, to fulfil his dreams and had already fallen in love... It seemed like a big mountain had suddenly propped up from somewhere, when all he wanted was to cross the river. That night somehow, he couldn't sleep; the way Lovleen smiled and moved, the way she sweetly behaved with all, all her traits had given rise to a new awareness within him, of which he had been ignorant till now. The world had suddenly become full of colors, music and laughter.

Over the days, he learnt that she was from a small village called Bahadurpur, a famous diary-farm-boasting pride, of the Punjab. The fuss her family had created on campus, when they had come, all of them together, clown-like almost, in their vibrant outfits and loud mannerisms, to get their girl admitted to the Girls' Hostel, had been a favorite topic of discussion and jokes for weeks later, amongst the students. They had giggled and nicknamed her "Ms.Peacock". The mention of her family, reminded him of his own, and he went over to the booth across the college, to make a call.

Every day, on his way from Hostel to College Campus, he had to pass a row of colony houses that belonged to the families of Retired

Army Personnel. He saw a middle-aged woman in one of those, daily, tending to her flowers with such care and passion, as if they meant the life to her...she reminded him of his own mother. Once, she called him over, "Hello dear, come in, I see you daily walking up to college."

They soon became close friends. Mrs. Batra told him by and by, of her late husband, Col. Harbhajan Batra, a fiery army officer, and her only son, a gallant Captain, (martyr of the Kargil War). She narrated, her eyes moist with memories, how he would bring her orchids from his various trips and posts, whenever he returned home. It was in cherish of his passion, that she loved her orchids so dearly. As he was about to leave, she pulled out a beautiful bloom and placed it on his palm saying, "Pass this onto your favorite someone today, as I have done!" she chuckled.

He thanked her, and hid it inside his haversack, skeptical of the bullies that abounded the campus, lest they would see it and create a new issue... (He had heard cases of ragging, and just couldn't understand what ragging was all about!?) He saw her sitting with her group, chatting loudly as was her typical style. He was happy for her that she had found company. He slipped up behind unnoticed, and slid the stem into her bag. When she entered class, he loved the look of her puzzled expression, as she scanned in all directions and flushed while she sat down. Though he was a good student, and needed no prompting to finish projects, studies were getting tougher. His roommate, as well as others in the batch, often involved him with problem-solving; which he obliged. Mrs. Batra had nearly adopted him as her foster son, often asking him to run her petty errands and daily gifting him a lovely flower on his way to college (which he would pass onto "her", in ways he invented on a daily basis), keeping fingers crossed lest she discovered him.

One afternoon, after classes, as he was leaving for hostel, he saw a circle of seniors with a new "catch", obviously. He had been tired with classes and the pressure the approaching examinations had brought he thought it was better to walk away; but the ethics of upbringing within him, didn't allow him to do so. He decided to exercise the principle of non-tolerance of violation, his town was known for.

He approached the battlement of bullies heroically, and was shocked to see Lovleen in the center-confused, helpless, and embarrassed to find herself in such a situation. He felt anguished beads of sweat trickle down his sideburns.

"Say it! Say it in Kannada, Ms. Peacock. Won't you spread your colorful feathers today?" a bully ordered. Another piped in, "Say" I love you" in Kannada and you can fly away birdie." Before he knew what he was doing, he had already stepped into the circle and had offered, "Take me in her place, and let her go." The leader of the shameless gang joked," The thepla will replace the bhatura and compete pongal!? Cluck Cluck!" initiating a round of applause. "Alright, come on, say it!"

"Nanu priti," he said calmly. "Nanu priti", he had repeated, to make their jaws drop lower. He noticed their reluctance to let them away. She too was speechlessness with amazement as she kept looking at him in gratitude and was fondly impressed. He held her hand and led her away. He felt as though the two of them had been bonded and deported to the outskirts of college, for the crime of loving each other. She had tears in her eyes, when she finally looked up in his eyes and thanked him, "Thank you ji, once again." He walked her up to her hostel too, silent yet with a thousand echoes of her words ringing within...

He had had a very pleasant morning, spending a tranquil time-almost meditative - hearing the murmurs of the orchids, swaying gracefully in the subtle, cool and aromatic breeze. Mrs. Batra had gifted him a pink bud today, "For unending love", she cheered sportingly.

As he thought of a chance, to pass it to her, how he wished he could just give it openly instead, with a kiss on her cheek. He set towards college quite enthusiastically. He saw her midway, just as luck would have it! And then with a blowing sweep, the mischievous wind snatched her dupatta and threw it onto the branches of a nearby tree. He saw her running after it, jumping as high as she could to untangle and rescue it from the forked clutches of the tree. He hurried forward to help her, just in time to witness the horror, as she lost her footing and slipped off the edge, into a tributary of the Cauvery, flowing uncomplainingly, unware of the unwelcome addition to it, gathered from the banks...

He wasted no time in diving in after her, yelling "Lovleen hold on! Lovleen! Lovleen here!" with all the power in his lungs. But the waves kept pulling her further away from him. He swam frantically, harder and faster, fighting the waves to reach her, until he caught her hand and had pulled her tightly against himself. He struggled a long while till he got them both safely ashore. He puffed and breathed fast, gasping and catching some air. He slapped and patted her lifeless form...frozen and immovable. And as if Cupid had a game ready for the day, he made Jaison's wish come true - he kissed her - trying to revive her with a mouth to mouth resuscitation, sucking water out of her lungs and nose. She vomited water, choked and coughed, coming to her senses. She remembered falling into the water, her rescuer's screams..." Thank you, ji" she managed to blurt incoherently, shaken and shivering. He wrapped her around her shoulders, with his own arms and led her away.

Passing the tree, he released her dupatta too and gave it to her. She smiled. She knew she no longer had to thank him. Whereas

146

he just thought of the morning and the pink bloom "For unending love".

The summer break forced most of the students to go back home. But it had been difficult for Jai this time, to wait for getting over with it; he so badly wanted to resume college. His family of course, mistook it as an addition to his sincerity towards his studies. He felt life returning to him only when he spotted her. She had come with a box in hand, and gave it to him, "Best milk sweets in the whole of Punjab, ji!" she offered with nostalgic pride, mixed with happiness at seeing him again. This was the third time, they had met after holidays, each time she brought him a sweet box from her "family-owned PC Dairy Farm". He returned the favor with a pair of bangles he had bought from the market, and had hidden in his trunk from family. She blushed while taking it...

She, however, could never solve the mystery of how an orchid, reached her daily, nor the identity of her "secret admirer"- as her friends had started teasing her. And so passed the days, as did Mrs. Batra too, one sultry day. Jaison took a few friends too with him, for her funeral rites, and did the part of a son in it. She had willed all her wealth to an orphanage, and a letter for Jaison. "Dear Jai, may these orchids always bloom and bring happiness in your life, as they did in mine", it read, and a bunch of orchids with it... He looked up when an aircraft passed above, and was happy for the union of the Batra family.

The Graduation Ceremony was soon approaching. He had bagged "The Student of the Year" trophy! Topper in three of the subjects passed, but she was nowhere to be found?! What became of her? He had been immediately employed on the basis of his merits, by a highly reputed firm.

How the years rolled on, the count of which was simply neglected solely, by the immersion of his time into his work. Years later, when he accidently bumped into few of his batch mates, he learnt she had been called away urgently by her family, and later married off, (against her wishes), to the son of a wealthy businessman. That was the last anyone had heard about her...

And now, here she had been, in this very cabinet! He walked into her cabinet, when everyone had gone for their lunch break. "Mrs. Lovleen Dhingra, General Manager", he read on the placard placed on her desk and smiled. But she did not appear to have a trace of the Lovleen he had known. Now soft-spoken, wearing a pastel sari, widowed mother of a ten-year-old. He placed the orchid he had brought from his vase, next to the placard and turned to leave.

She was standing at the doorway, observing him intently. How the whole jigsaw puzzle started fitting, piece by piece in her mind. She blushed on seeing him. He abruptly stood still too, seeing her. It was her, who walked up to him slowly, put a hand lightly on his shoulder and whispered "Nanu priti, ji." He smiled and blushed sweetly. She continued, "Nothing else for now, but just tell me this, how did you know the translation?" "Oh, you see, it was quite simple actually. My roommate Parimal, had a Kannada girlfriend, whose photo he'd keep below his pillow, and every bedtime, speak a thousand endearments to it- "Nanu priti" being the oft repeated one." He smiled and continued, in a lower voice, "And can you guess, whom I would think of, when he would say those words?" It was her turn to blush again.

He held her hand in his, the touch bringing back the days he had thought were gone, and led her away, just as he had twenty years ago. He knew the taste of the milk sweets would never leave him now! And as though reading his mind, she had confirmed with a shy nod, as if they were saying it with all the countless orchids that exchanged hands between them...

So now, dear readers, you have taken the demonstration, the complete tour of the coconut farms, the dairy farms, the orchid garden, and so the class adjourned-go home and wish you all a happy recipe trying!

Do say it with orchids - "Nanu priti"!

Elora Rath

Apart from being an author, Elora Rath juggles her life between PhD and job search. Hailing from the small township of Dhenkanal, she moved to the temple city Bhubaneswar with her family for a better career and life. She comprehends her innate urge and creative passion towards writing is solely inherited from her mother who rejoiced liberal arts as a medium of expression of her thoughts. She considers writing as her soul talk. Apart from writing in various languages and forms, to ink her emotions on sheets, she also has a keen interest of indulging herself in dancing, singing, photography, travelling, internet surfing and cooking in her free time. She believes life taught her more than what she could ever have learnt from a very tender age and the reflections of which can be traced in her writing which picks up delicate issues and small charms of human relationships as a core concern.

A real life modern relationship article of hers has been featured in the book called "21 Things about Romance" by Grapevine India Publisher. She has contributed and got selected to be part of 20 other anthologies by now. Her debut novel "I never expected... Life would change so much!" released pan India on April 21st 2015. Being an avid reader, follower of Cricket, binge watcher of movies and TV series, she finds herself incriminated in the above mentioned guilty pleasures when she gets a break from work.

She can be contacted at – rath.elora@gmail.com

Facebook - https://www.facebook.com/elora89

Twitter - https://twitter.com/elorarath

Gmail - rath.elora@gmail.com

10

THAT'S HOW LIFE IS...

Elora Rath

"Mumma, can I please go out and play?" asked Sameer, her five year old son, all geared up to play bat ball with the neighbourhood kids, standing at the kitchen door for permission, soon after having lunch.

"No baby, it's very sunny outside and you just had lunch. It's not good for health to play just after lunch. So now I want my rock star to catch up some nap and rest for a while. I promise to wake you up around 5 in evening and then you can go out to play for as long as you wish. Now just hug Mumma and go to sleep like a good boy", said Sheetal while doing the dishes in the kitchen and looking at Sameer in the middle of the dishes. His face fell listening to her.

"Please Mumma, all my friends are coming. Nitin has bought a new bat ball set and we all will be playing a match now. I am the captain of my cricket team Mumma, I can't stay back home. Please let me go else they will think I am afraid to be hit by the ball. I won't play in the sun and will drink a lot of water too. See, I have taken my water bottle and we will play inside the club house. Let me go Mumma, please", plead little Sameer putting his Mickey Mouse cap on head to complete his sportsman look.

"But beta, it's not healthy to play immediately after having food and you must be tired after school. You need to sleep else you would doze off early in the evening without doing homework and that's not the sign of a good boy. Teacher will punish you tomorrow for not doing homework and I don't want my boy to get scolded. So hurry up and go to bed now", told Sheetal lovingly with a little commanding tone reflecting her sternness.

"But Mumma…"

Before Sheetal could deny him again, her parents emerged from the guest room and asked little Sameer to go out to play but advising him to playing in the club house avoiding the hot sun; their club house had enough space for little Tendulkars to hit boundaries and sixes. Sameer elated with an ear to ear smile, jumped off the sofa bed and ran to hug his grandma uttering that he was convincing Mumma by saying the same thing but she was in no mood to listen. Blowing an air kiss to Mumma and giving high five to grandpa, Sameer went out of the door ever so excited. Sheetal looked displeased but did not say anything to her parents as the old couple adored Sameer to the fullest, granted his every wish and were also experienced parents who knew better about dealing with kids.

"Are you done with dishes my dear or you need any help?" her mother Padma asked from the hall sitting with her husband Ashok who was watching some wild life conservation activities discovery channel.

"No Mom, I am done with the dishes. Will you both like to have some coffee? I am thinking of brewing a cup for me," voiced Sheetal still from the kitchen, now busy with the coffee maker.

"Sounds good darling, bring two more cups and then we will watch some classic over the DVD player. Your dad got some yesterday from Ravin's video parlour. Dad said that Ravin was asking about you, after all you were friends from childhood. He was asking about Sameer too. Such a gentleman he is. You know the other day he also helped us in the vegetable market, seeing me struggling with two bags full of vegetables and fruits. He is a really nice guy", uttered Padma hinting the conversation in the angle Sheetal never wished to talk.

In the kitchen, Sheetal gave a displeased look, knowing that the age old conversation had started again, it would stretch for hours, upsetting, disturbing and frustrating her, also draining her emotionally days together.

Sheetal remained silent whilst the coffee making was in progress. How many times had she asked Mom not to raise the topic but she just did not listen! Ravin was a great guy, was her classmate since kindergarten days and a really close friend but that's all. She had never seen him in that context even after knowing that he had a big crush on her since standard seven when both of them played the role of "Heer and Ranjha" – the eternal lovers in a school play. Ravin's emotions had got entangled with Sheetal's nonchalant attitude towards him which led to circumstances that they hardly spoke face to face in the many years and that abruptly severed a long friendship. Ravin got married years before her wedlock but was now a divorcee and a father of two. His wife found her soul mate in her school time sweetheart and she chose to dump him and start a family of their own stating that its only one life and one should spend it with the one his/her heart calls for. Ravin, as a father was doing great for his two daughters who are in school now. But still, she never felt the urge to change the equation of their relationship. Friendship is the only thing she could offer him, nothing else but who can convince that to Mom who choose to act as a match maker all the time as if it would fetch her some international accolades or something. Never mind!

Mom and Dad were still glued to TV when Sheetal entered the living room with three cups of coffee. Everyone picked their mugs and she sat comfortably on the bean bag enjoying her cup. Mom cleared her throat and asked, "Sheetal, enough of all this hide and seek. We want to know when are you thinking of re-marrying. We are here since a week but you are avoiding our questions deliberately. We are not forcing you for anything but think rationally. We are aging, Sameer is growing up and you are all alone with a private job that has no guarantee. How will you handle things once he grows up, financially and otherwise? Don't you think Sammer needs a father too? And what about you dear, you are just 29. Will you spend all your life alone being a single mother?" questioned an anxious Padma to her only daughter who seemed to ignore all her prattle and concentrate more on her coffee and TV.

"Ashok, I am done with this girl. Look at her, now she has become such a grown up girl that she prefers not to answer me. What wrong have I done? I am concerned about her and my Sameer but she thinks this over thinking and over protective mother of her has lost her mind. I can't bear this silence anymore. My daughter is suffering every moment but I can't do anything about it. Oh God, what should I do?"

Padma left the room in tears cursing her fate. Ashok stroked Sheetal's hair and gestured her to stay calm. He also got up to leave but before that he looked lovingly at Sheetal and said, "You know darling, in the process of being independent and strong, we at times lose the vulnerability and innocence that once personified us. Every person needs a companion at certain point of life on whom we can rely. Life partner shares life, its smiles and sorrows, promises and pasts, failures and futures. Without someone to hold your hand in downfalls and rises to celebrate life, it's just a waste. So think about it." Dad left to console mom and Sheetal kept thinking about the words spoken by him till the coffee lost its warmth.

The evening went as silently as the dinner, except Sameer's endless jabber about how he hit countless sixes in his afternoon cricket match. Grandma and grandpa retired to their room after wishing Sameer good night. Sheetal asked Sameer to finish his homework while she finished all the odd jobs in kitchen. Around 10.30, Sheetal dragged Sameer from front of the TV and put him to bed. Sheetal crawled on the bed and Sameer placed his left arm on her. She smiled and kissed her son. Sameer pointed at the photo frame kept on side table and asked, "Mumma, when is papa coming?"

"Soon baby, now go to sleep", Sheetal said while caressing his hair.

"Papa is looking nice in the shirt; Mumma I need a same shirt like him for Diwali; tell papa to bring the same styled shirt for me. I will look cool" said Sameer eyes muffled in sleep.

Sheetal did not utter a word, patting Sameer gently, tears rolled down her eyes as she picked up the photo frame and looked at her husband who smiled candidly. The memories of that fateful day flashed in front of her eyes...

It was August 13th, 2009. The downpour has stopped for a while. The sky was still covered with dark clouds and rainbows were visible on the skyline enhancing the beauty of an otherwise greyish sky. She was nine months and few days pregnant then. Her delivery date was very near may be in a day or two. Three house helps were appointed at home to take care of her. Her husband was extremely careful about her and their baby. It was their first child. They both were extremely happy as well as anxious. She could remember the day when he had come to see her at home for their alliance. It was an arranged marriage. She was apprehensive to meet and marry a stranger which he sensed after seeing her discomfort. When they were asked to talk privately, he admitted that he liked her but wanted her opinion. He also stated that if it's okay for her to marry him, then they should date like couples in love, so that they don't miss out on the fun and gain the idea about each other's lifestyle. She agreed to the proposal not just because he looked nice but his mentality too seemed to match her idea of a perfect guy. He was just the way she wanted her would-be husband to be. They dated for four months before getting engaged. Their parents were upbeat just like them. They got married few months later and life became a bliss. She could have never imagined she would find a guy who loved her insanely. His world revolves around her and he was the centre of universe for her. A year passed and he got pregnant. God had gifted them the most beautiful feeling in the world, parenthood. She felt like the luckiest woman in the world.

Ond day she had woken up from a bad dream. Her head was spinning lightly and a persistent ache hurting her forehead. She found herself on her master bed with a few of books, hair band and clips, diary and reading glass lying aside. She picked up the glass full of water from the side table and drank it in one go. Her throbbing heart still needed some time to calm down after that dream." Argh! That was not funny at all", she thought. "God, why am I seeing the same dangerous dream from last few months? It's goddamn frightening." Pregnancy makes one feeble, fragile and vulnerable but still a constant dreadful dream almost every day was not any common thing that she heard happens during pregnancy. She was tensed and it showed on her face, forming a few lines of worry on her forehead.

Uneasily, she stepped down of the bed and walked up to the window. Opening the soft satin curtains with her hands, she felt the gush of misty air squeezing into the room, stroking her face gently making her smile with the sway of cold breezes playing along with her hair. Sprinkles of rain droplets over her face tickled her skin. It was early evening and she realized that she had slept off the entire afternoon with a book in hand and her study glasses on head, tired. Tying the lock of her thick black hair into a bun, she yawned and stretched her hands to relax and adjust. Just then a pair of hand moved around her belly button from sides of her waist, caressing her mildly with the finger tips touching slowly her bare skin. She knew Shekhar and his ever so romantic self could not stay apart from her even for a second when he was home. Shekhar rested his face on her shoulder and they enjoyed the calmness of the picturesque golden-orange painted horizon. He kissed her earlobes slowly, which continued to a full-fledged french kiss and ended up in a bear hug. Enjoying the hot streaming cups of coffee in their terrace garden, Shekhar noticed the hint of sadness in Sheetal's eyes. Sheetal told him about pregnancy woes and work related stress, avoiding the actual reason as she knew Shekhar would laugh it off the second he would hear about it! Taking Sheetal into his warm embrace, Shekhar matter-of-factually said, "Look Jaan, if the work is distressing you and you are not happy with it, then you better quit and look for some change. How many times have I asked you not to work in this state, even if it's from home? I know you are independent and you want to be that way. And I love and respect that about you. But I cannot see you like this. Since last few days you are so lost in your own thoughts. You are not even excited about things you love, not even chocolates. I know how much you love them." Sheetal was just looking at him without a blink. Shekhar continued, "See I love your smile and that is the first thing I want to notice, when I am home. It just makes my day. Our house looks brighter, happier and worth-living when you look at me in that hale and hearty smile." Sheetal smiled to his charming boyish remark. "How could she be so lucky to end up with a man who loves and dots her like crazy" She thought.

"Baby, let's go out tonight like for a candle light dinner and a long drive. I feel like we have not done something like that for years", said Shekhar enthusiastically.

"Shekhar, don't you think you sometimes forget that you are going to be Papa in real, like maximum in a week's time. How can I go out sweet heart, I feel dizzy most of the time. And even I don't feel like having any spicy food at any crowed place. I just want you, me and a quiet dinner under that stars. I want to sleep in your arms and please no office work related calls tonight. I am fed up with your work. I want some alone time with you", told Sheetal looking at his face.

"Okay honey, I am at your service tonight and no one can disturb us. Let me just freshen up then", told Shekhar while going inside the bathroom while Sheetal was still in the balcony enjoying the rains. It was a perfect weather to pre-celebrate the arrival of the new member to their family.

It was 8 at night. Table was set. The ambience was chilly. The twinkling lights were illuminating the area with hues of gold, red and green. The moon was hiding behind the dark patches of clouds, the stars were blurry and the sky did not exactly give a romantic feel but the adamant couple were sure to make the night a memorable one. Shekhar guided her to the rocking chair and helped her in parching herself on it. He handed her a glass of lemonade and made himself comfortable in the chair next to her. He held her hand in his while sipping his mocktail and said, "Darling, finally I have decided the name of my baby, if it's a girl, Sameera and if it's a boy, Sameer. Aren't the names cute?" "But Shekhar, they are such common names. I want my kid to have a unique name. How about Nirvan or Swastika?" said Sheetal. "Are you planning to make my kids saints in future or what? What's with such spiritual names? I guess you are watching too many devotional channels now a days. No wonder how such names are coming to your head. It's the names I decide are final" said Shekhar sternly. "Okay tell me the reason why Sameer or Sameera, then I will decide. After all the baby is within me so I have the right to have the last word in the say" said Sheetal. "Sameer means the breath of fresh air and that's what our baby is for us, a positive and productive change, a new bundle of emotions and happiness so Sameer or Sameera." "I agree, it will be Sameer or Sameera then, let God decide who would fill our world in joy" prayed Sheetal in heart.

The dinner was served on the table. Shekhar held her hand and made her sit on the dinning chair. The candles were burning so was passion in their eyes. She tasted the food which satisfied her taste bud and ignited the appetite. She smiled. He smiled. Candles burnt lighting up the ambience. They were done with the dinner and he was walking her to bed but she denied saying she had slept long in afternoon and after dinner, feeling little suffocated so wanted to spend some time in open air. He agreed and arranged for the recliner to have a comfortable sleep. She was resting in his arms; he was looking at her with love. The whisk of cool air blew in furry and inside the duvet, the couple were keeping themselves warm. She suddenly noticed his shirt, the one she had got him for his last birthday, a royal blue one which suited his skin tone and made him look as dashing as ever. "Baby, I am tired of this blue shirt. How many times will you wear this? I mean on every date we plan, you wear the same shirt as if it's the only shirt you have" said Sheetal. "But I thought you love me in this shirt. You said I look really nice in it. It's gifted by you, so it's special. I won't take it off now. It's cold out here and you can molest me too" replied Shekhar cracking the joke. Sheetal looked a bit tensed remembering the dream but ignoring it, she pressed her head in Shekhar's chest to sleep.

Minutes later she began to feel an unbearable pain in her lower abdomen. She squeezed Shekhar's hand tightly and he understood something was wrong with her. She was sweating heavily, screaming in pain. His mind had gone blank in a moment seeing some blood mixed with some liquid flowing down her dress wetting the recliner and ground. He quickly called up the gynaecologist and detailed her everything. He advised him to bring Sheetal to hospital as soon as possible mentioning that her water just had broken. He called for the house helps and asked them to look after Sheetal while he fidgeted with his phone connecting to their driver who had left for home after dropping him in the evening. Shekhar did not know how to drive and there was nobody who could help him at home. He dialled for the ambulance and looked for his neighbour on the same floor. To their bad luck, nobody was available there who knew driving. The rains had started pouring mightily and now the building lift was not functioning due to power failure. The storm began in such a way that the mobile phones showed no network in a matter of few minutes. Shekhar came back to Sheetal who was in the bedroom now crying in severe pain. He took her hand in his and asked her to calm down. He looked exactly the same as she saw him in her dreadful dreams, nervous, anxious, emotional and sweaty. He told her he would be back any moment and that he was going downstairs to arrange for a taxi. But she clutched his shirt begging him not to leave her alone. He caressed her cheeks, kissed her forehead and placed his hand on her belly saying that they cannot wait more, it can affect the baby, just as she saw in her dream. She was perplexed and fearful if the dream turns true. She hugged him and asked him not to go out but he did not listen to her, for him the lives of his wife and his kid were at risk. They were damn important than any stupid circumstances. He began to move, she screamed his name. He looked back at his wife struggling in pain. Tears flew down his eyes. She asked him to change the shirt to which he got confused but ignoring her words thinking them to be the in fits of delivery pains, he strode down the stairs nimbly.

She was screaming his name. The maids were getting frightened of her wildness. The rains had subsided. The sky seemed cleared but there was no sign of Shekhar after fifteen minutes. Ward boys rushed to their bed room with a stretcher and made her shift to it. With tad difficulty, they came down the four storey building. By that time, Sheetal had lost her senses and the night was over before she could open her eyes.

She was lying on the hospital bed still unconscious when their parents reached. They were paranoid obviously not knowing how to react and face Sheetal. She woke up around 11 in the morning as she was given sedatives, opened her eyes and her first look fell on her and Shekhar's parents who had tears in eyes and smiles on their lips. She was confused. Mom came close to her and sat on her bed. She asked her to look at the pram kept aside her bed where a newly born baby boy was sleeping peacefully. She looked at her mother in amazement and her mother in law handed her the baby. She looked at the new born and his face reminded her of Shekhar. The baby boy resembled him, the same eyes, same round face but where was Shekhar? When she asked the same to their parents, they had no answers to give. The sight of her dreams started hovering in her mind, her hands trembled and in time, her mother got hold of the little baby else he could have got hurt. Sheetal's gazes probed in to both the parent's eyes which were avoiding her. Her hands were getting cold. Her heart was throbbing insanely as if it would come out of the skin with a big thrust. She felt nauseated as if she is going to faint. Her head spun making her surrounding seem like moving around her. She felt dizzy. Her eye lids felt heavy. Before shutting her eyes, she asked for Shekhar who was nowhere to be seen. Her parents held her strongly before she crashed to bed unconscious. Sheetal stayed in hospital for another three days when she was informed that Shekhar was no more. In that storming night when he ran across the road to ask for a taxi, a rash driven truck hit him in the side of the road. He died on the spot. Sheetal could not believe what she heard. Her brutal dream came true which shook her up. She begged her parent's to look at the dead body of Shekhar once. When she saw him in the mortuary, it killed her within. Her heart bled to death. She was numb. She was speechless. Her emotions were dead. She felt guilty for his death and the shirt she had always seen in her dreams still adorn his body with blotches of blood in it. She cursed herself of not sharing her dreams with anyone; at least someone would have understood her. She was in a state where neither she could smile or cry heartily. She was in the threshold of emotional turbulence when losing mind appeared to be easier than behaving rationally.

"Almost five years passed by. Now Sameer has begun to go to school. He has features almost similar to you and he loves me a lot just like you love me. He sleeps cuddling me just like you used to. He loves you and always asks to speak to you as I had told him that you are at some faraway place cruising in the ocean where there is no network. He looks at your photos and says that he would be like you someday. He is a kid but he understands me well, without saying a word. You said it right; Sameer is the breath of fresh air. He came to my life when you abruptly left. I would have died a thousand deaths if he had not been clung to my chest. In him, I found a reason to live. Without you, it's difficult yet I smile. I remember our unforgettable memories of the time we spent together, be it for a short span but those moments give me strength that somewhere you are still with me and protecting both of us like you had always done. I love you Shekhar, you were the best thing that happened to me and for you only Sameer is in my arms now, the most pleasant gift of our togetherness. You know mom was telling about Ravin today but how come she never understands that we were soul mates who need no other person to complete us. I have you and Sameer and that's my family. May be you are not here in person, but are in my every heartbeat. I miss you love", spoke Sheetal to the old photo frame of them together taken at the terrace whilst celebrating Shekhar's first birthday with her. Her parents were listening to her conversation with her departed husband and tears rolled down the eyes of the old couple seeing still how madly their daughter was in love with Shekhar. They left for their room. Sheetal kissed the photo, wished good night and retired to sleep cuddling her son in arms.

Memories are beautiful. Sheetal knew she has to live with the memories only but she was content that those memories were enough for her to live for next seven births. Life is all about memories that get accumulated as we live. Memories can make you, break you or bring out the best in you. Life is nothing but a basket of good, bad, unforgettable memories. That's how life is…unpredictable yet memorable.

J. Alchem

J. Alchem is a voracious reader and has a deep interest in the literature. He has done his post graduation (MBA) in Finance and International Business. He is the resident of India and residing in New Delhi. He has written in several local magazines and newspapers and received the appreciation for the same. He is actively involved in writing quotes and short write-ups in his Facebook page.

He is a winner of Storytelling contest (ranked 3rdbest story teller) organized by Dr. Amit Nagpal. His quotes are seen being circulated among the youth in Facebook, Whatsapp and other Social networking sites, which is a reward to him by his readers. His stories have been published in numerous Anthologies (such as the second life, Blank Space, Love Bytes, Mighty Thoughts etc.) and online websites.

Presently, he is looking for a traditional publisher for his book; "A Road not travelled?" meanwhile, he is working (researching) on his next book.

Contacts details:

Facebook page- www.facebook.com/JAlchem

Email id- alchemj@gmail.com

11

CATHERINE

J Alchem

I am a 42 year old doctor who is practicing as a Psychologist and Neurologist from the last 15 years. In these 15 years I have seen various types of patient in my hospital. Having the urge to jump from the roof, to burn themselves alive or even jump in front of the train, some patients were suffering from suicidal tendencies. Some suffered from the sleeping disorders, whenever they went to sleep, they felt like someone was hiding just beneath the bed and going to strangulate them etc.

From all over America, strange cases came to me and I successfully solved all of them with my experience, with my medicines and with my unique way to feel their life, indulge myself in their mess and take out a solution for their problem.

But there was a case which I could never forget. A case I have never ever imagined in my life and no book ever taught me about, it was indeed a unique case. When I was leaving for my home from the hospital, I got a call from someone in Alaska.

"Is it doctor Rusenvelt?" the voice asked over the phone.

"Yes, who is this?" I asked the strange man, although I knew it was of surely of patient. I never make a fuss when a patient contacts me or tries to meet me in the odd hours. It is the duty of a doctor to take every patient on the instant whenever they arrive.

"I am Nicholas, l" he replied over the phone after a pause.

"Yes, how I can help you?" I replied while adjusting the paper weight on the table.

"Do you know Nicholas Sieum?" he asked.

"Nicholas Sieum? The author?" I inquired.

Nicholas Sieum was a best seller author of epic books. So far he had written 5 novels love stories and all of them were best sellers. I wasa big fan of his. Whenever his book arrived on the amazon.com as a pre order, I always rushed to the internet to make an order and in 3 days I devoured all the words of the novel in my heart despite my busy schedule. I later repent on this behavior of mine because once I complete the novel, I do not have much to read. Then I re-read the novel, over and over again n. I highlight my favorite parts and sometimes I even speak them out lous. It is not only me who is the fan of his epic novels but my wife too. Most nights we read the tales of love spun by him, before going to bed.

I have to confess, most of the romance in my life, I have borrowed from the concoctions of love stirred by him. I even went on to suggest his books to my friends, relatives and even to my patients sometimes. They too loved it. I do not think there is any reader who does not know about him. Even the movie-goers know of him, considering the fact that four of his novels had been turned into movies for non-reasers' sakes. "Yes, I am his father" the man replied over the phone.

"Delighted to talk with you sir, how are you?" I asked in a single breath. The paper weight slipped from my hand and touched the corner of the table as soon as he introduced himself to me.

"It is about my son Nicholas Sieum, I wanted to meet you," his tone bothered me.

"Yeah yeah! Sure sir" I replied with a joy of meeting such a great celebrity and personality but at the same time, I realized the graveness in his voice and chided myself mentally of my prior excitement. After checking my schedule, I said into the phone, "Tomorrow after 9?" "Ok, see you then," he said and hung up the phone.

I took the keys of my car and moved towards the parking lot. I never liked the idea of having a driver. Never could fathom why one would hire a driver to enjoy the pleasure of using an expensive car with a ravishing engine. The car was meant for me. With that thought, I started the engine.

Next day at exactly 9 o' clock I was at the home of Nicholas Sieum. There Nicholas Will welcomed me with a slight smile and took me inside a his library slash study. There were thousands of book there and obviouslyI felt great to be there. After all these were the books dear to Nicholas Sieum. how could I school my mind. His father made me siton a beautiful leather sofa.

"My son is is in love," he told me."Alright…" I replied shifting my eyes from the shelves to him. "This is the problem," he added.

"Is it? Being in love is good I think, and he is certainly good at spinning stories about it, he must be good at it," I ventured, not relly sure where this was heading. "Yeah it is good but with whom he is in love with, is the root of the problem," he said, making circles on the surface of the sofa. For all I knew I may have been called there for idle chatter.

I wanted to ask "With whom?" but I did not. So I waited.

He looked straight in my eye before stating, "He is in love with Catherine."

My mind raced at the sound of the name as I recollected how each of his novel featured a love interest by the name of Catherine.

In each of his book three things are constant: One is the female character: Catherine. Second is Amay: the male character and the third thing was, of course, Romance I am that much fond of his book, that I had begun to call my wife Catherine. It always brought a smile to her face.

Catherine was a 24 years old girl, 5'6" in height, fair complexion, brown hair scattered over her face like sky turned brown to give glow to the moon, cheeks like winter apple, little green eyes like the nature lives there, and a long nose like a way to go to heaven. She was perfect in her body but there was only one thing on her face which was odd, and it was a cut mark on the forehead "So finally, he met his Catherine," I don't know if I asked him or I merely stated the fact. He became restless, unable to find his word.

"He is in love with the Catherine of his book, she is a fictional character," he finally said. Everything lost its way. My mind, my eyes, my ears, and my thoughts everything, just my heart was beating with a pace and discovering the emotion of how to react. I was completely in shock. The room felt hot despite the air-conditioning. "Catherine?" I said, with a lump forming in my throat. I could not comprehend. "How did this happen?' I asked "I do not know. You are a reader of his book. He every time thinks to make good love story between Amay and Catherine and in this it went so much in deep to Catherine that he regarded her as a real character, nowadays he even see her in his dreams. He calls her name…." his father went on and on and on about what just had happened.

He showed me the room of Nicholas Sieum where I found so many books here and there. At the table many rough notes about the Catherine, on the wall portray of her, her beauty, her character like a professional painter discovering his muse.

I discovered the antiques pieces belongs to the Catherine in the fictions, the wrist watch he portrayed in his book. The purse she carries most of the time, her pair of sandals. Her moon shaped ear rings, her lipsticks brand, her favorite movies DVD, her bracelets, and every tiny thing about her there.

Now I discovered how he portrays her so live picture in his writing, told every accessory she carries so closely. It was clear looking like that the room was not belongs to him but to Catherine. The same room I knew while reading in his book.

Even I felt like the Catherine is real character just by founding her outfits, her belongings here and there. It was hard to believe that the character is fictional even for me as it was looking like he knew Catherine well. He is friend of her. She comes to meet him and some of her belongings are here.

How smartly he collected everything of her or how smartly he bought the things and made them of her fictional character of Catherine.

It was strange and shocking moment for me as I was a fond reader of his writing so I understood the chemistry behind his love story in the book as well as in the real. How he just regarded the fictional character as a real.

Then his father took me to the room and handed me a piles of later. I checked them one by one. I opened them and made myself amazed. Those were the letters he wrote to Catherine and posted to her but they returned back to the main address because there was no existence of that address he wrote, so postman dropped them here.

I read many of them. I fell in love with his letters. In every love letter of him he was behaving like a child, like he is a child and looking for his lover with whom he can spend his time forever.

"My love

Catherine

Three months passed away but you did not reply of any of my letters, I do not know why? I wrote the correct address all the time over my letter. I even told you how much I love you. I do

169

not expect that you should also fall in love with me and marry me but I want to tell you, I love you beyond any boundation rule, regulation and society, and even beyond my breath. I everyday see you in my dreams. I everyday tell you how much I love you and you every day smiles and passes away from my sight without saying even a single word. I lost in your smile like I forgot everything of life, like I forgot my existence.

I am more than me when you are around.

I am more than free when you are around.

You are the only one who makes me complete.

I am actually more than complete when you are around.

I feel like I am just a soul, Nobody is around me when you are not around.

Catherine, this is my 16th letter to you.

With a hope, one day, you will fall in love with me too.

Ever's yours'
Nicholas Sieum

It made me little bit emotional. How a person can be in love with someone so deeply even when there is no existence of her.

I remember the days when my wife was pregnant. I was attached to our child too much, every day before going to hospital I kiss at her belly to my child and when I return from the office, I do the same. And then one day, my wife fell from the stairs and the child lost his life before coming in existence. That day we both wept a lot. Whenever I remember about my child, it brings the tears in my eyes.

But Nicholas's love is totally different. He even did not see her presence in the real but still he loves her more than anything. How could be a person such a lovely that even not being in existence make others fall in love.

A tear rolled down over my cheeks and I successfully hid it from his father.

We moved to the terrace and talked about this. He told me how they just discovered this love of him and how much attach he is with Catherine.

"Sometime he even comes to me, puts his head in my lap and cry- cry- and cry. And when I ask the reason, he told me how much he loves Catherine. When I tell him that I will talk to Catherine to putt his tears off. He denies me to do that, "no papa, I did not love her with a condition that I will own her. I love her because I fell for her. I own her soul. It is around me all the time. These tears are not for the reason she is not around but because she is much around Papa. Papa she is much around." Nicholas Will told me and went silent. Tears dropped from his eyes and he wiped them off by tissue paper.

"He is my only son! Please help us" he put down his hands over my knee and pleaded.

I took his hands in mine.

"Don't worry, whatever I could do, I will" I replied with a little smile to wipe his tears indirectly.

I told him, 'I will' but I was still unaware of 'how?' the whole way to home I just thought about this different kind of case. Thinking about this extremely different love story.

"What happened?" my wife asked as soon as I entered into house. The best thing about the woman is that, you do not need to tell anything to them, they just figure it out on their own just by looking at your expression. They are the natural body language readers actually.

She came to me, removed my neck tie, kissed over my cheeks and I told her everything. I told her the complete story.

"How it can be? How a person can fall in love with a fictional character?" it was her first question while making the table for the lunch.

"From the last twelve years, his imaginations are moving around Catherine. To develop the reality in the character, he lived the moment with the Catherine, he covertly spent the time with her, talked to her, had a conversation with her, asked her hobbies, interest, lived with her behave, enjoyed her attitude and these imagination of him of 12 years made him believe that the Catherine is not a fictional character. His mind in the state that he is unable to separate the fictional character of Catherine from the real world" I told her as she put down the bowl of fruits on the table and set near me looking at me.

"So he believes, she is around" she asked me putting the plate of vegetable towards me.

"Yes and it's the problem. He is in a kind of illusion that his mind is not helping him to separate the both fiction and nonfiction" I replied.

"You man are really strange. You seem much strong from outside but from inside you are that much weak"

"What you are going to do now?" she asked looking at my face.

"First I will meet him tomorrow then I will decide what to do after looking at his condition closely." I replied

"I am with you" she put down her hand over my shoulder.

"He is doctor Rusenvelt" his father introduced me to him.

He was on his bed looking at the wall where he portrayed the picture of Catherine. He was looking at the wall like he was waiting for the Catherine to come alive in front of him. He saw me for a moment and then turned his sight on the wall again. He was looking different what he looks over the page of his books. Dark circle around eyes, subtle at face, lips were little bit dried and clothes were crumpled. He was completely in a mess like just he has discovered his own world somewhere else behind the wall. Here is just his body, his soul actually belongs to somewhere else far from here. Perhaps in the world of his own novel. Perhaps where the Catherine lives.

I set down nearby him, put down my hand over his shoulder. He felt it and then moved a bit aside from me.

"He is good man Sieum" his father spoke and I winked him to be silent.

I set there for around 10 minutes looking here and there the way he was looking and then I came out of the room.

"Will he be alright doctor?" his father asked to me with the wrinkles of worry over his forehead as soon as I came out of the room.

"I believe so" I replied after a pause of thought.

We doctor say this word all the times, sometime even when we do not believe in it personally just to give relief to the beating heart in worry.

Next full week I was busy in this strange kind of case. I decided to go far on this case and I mix all of the experience of mine. Finally I approached to Nicholas with the medicines and a way to put him apart from the fictional character. I told his father to give the pill so that he can fight with his illusion. I told them to keep him far from the home where the belongings of Catherine lying. I told them to keep him far from writing but it was Impossible to keep a writer far from his life. So I made a plan for that. I asked to one of my friend who was a well known publisher to put a contract with the Nicholas Sieum to write a novel for him with pre decided character. He approached him and gave him the list of the character he wanted in his books and thankfully to God Nicholas Sieum accepted the challenge.

There is good thing about the writer they just don't write the simple project sometime they make impossible possible by writing about it. They are the greatest creature of the God. They are the one who makes the life easy, valuable and worth living.

I believe if there is anything to fall in love in this world. Then it is falling in love with the books. They are the best companion. They are the best friend. You can open them at any time, look on them, learn from them, and fall in love with them. They do not disturb you, don't bother you. Whenever you want them, they are around. They do not have expectation from you. They do not feel awkward when you are not around. Whenever wherever you need them, they are there waiting for you to make you fall in love.

His father shifted the Nicholas Sieum to the Washington for the treatment of him as I asked to them where he was on the pills and special therapy of mine, far from the world of Catherine and his previous novel, writing a love story around other character.

His treatment went for around three month. Every week I too visit personally to know the condition of him and thankfully to god it was changing. He was feeling improvement. He was recovering from his illusion.

"How are you man?" I asked him while shaking hand. He was writing something on the paper. A usual job for a writer.

"Pretty well" he replied putting his diary aside with a glittering smile.

"May I see it" I asked after a formal conversation while pointing towards the dairy.

As I was his doctor, friend of his publisher so he did not denied me and gave the dairy to me. I turned many page of it and tried to look at the glimpse of Catherine there but she was not there.

"She was not" I jumped inside me with a joy that everything was going well. He was recovering from the illusion of his own fictional character.

"Nice words" I said after referring to a paragraph to hide my joy of success.

"These are not the word. These are the drops of blood. I die for writing to live in my story" he replied with a smile while taking the notebook from me.

I had conversation with Nicholas Will too about it and they thanked me a lot for the fastest recovery of him. I welcomed them and leaved for my home.

6 months later I received another call from the Nicholas Will.

"How are you Doctor Rusenvelt?" he asked as soon as I took the receiver to my hand.

"Hey! I am absolutely fine. How's going on?" I figure it out his voice.

"Good, I want to meet you" he spoke while shifting the receiver to another hand of him.

"Is everything alright?" I asked with a little worry although I knew whenever a doctor receives a call from someone. It is about 'not well'.

When people are well they do not make a call to thank the doctor. Seriously they don't. We doctor not only gives the pills to our patients but also pray for their better and fast recovery. So at least we deserve a feedback, a 'thank you' note but patients does not care most of the time, so we too.

"You should see it. Come here tomorrow" he replied after a long breath.

"Ok, I will come tomorrow" I replied with a strangeness of the matter.

Next day I reached Washington and met Nicholas Will there. He welcomed me and directly took me to the room of Nicholas Sieum without speaking a single word.

As soon as I entered into the room. My eyes turned round. Mouth became wide open, tongue hang in between. Saliva refused to go to neck back. I felt like heart is shifting just downward a little bit with the lubb dubb.

The whole room was different. Portray on the wall of the male character of his book: Amay. Things belongs to Amay were lying here and there. His wrist watch, his iconic Adidas shoes, his white and violet color scarf, his sunglasses of blue shades, his leather jacket carved "A" over the pocket of it. His denim jeans, his bowler hat. Everything ever belonged to the character to the Amay were there. A portray of the Amay on the wall and in front of the wall, a bad where Nicholas Sieum was set down looking and staring at the wall. He was completely in a mess like just he has discovered his own world somewhere else behind the wall. Here is just his body, his soul actually belongs to somewhere else far from here. Perhaps in the world of his own novel. Perhaps where the Amay lives.

He developed another kind of illusion now. He was Catherine now. He was Catherine.

Shreya Singh

Shreya, 18, from the holy city, Varanasi has recently completed her higher secondary classes and is about to join college for an engineering course. She has keeninterest in reading and loves to indulge herself in reading romantic stuffs.

She is very passionate about reading and writing. She is full of exuberant joy. She is witty and has got obnoxious humor and always fascinated by deepness of philosophical nature of human being. In the near future, she visualizes herself busy with her studies and wantsto devote rest of her life to writing and reading.

You can reach her at - Shreya.singhjeet@gmail.com

12

HE LIVES IN ME

Shreya Singh

It was a scorching hot sunny day filled with a chilled breeze; weird combination. I was incapable of judging the weather, and even more incapable of judging the next moment of my life. It was an arduous choice between sitting infront of PC, waiting for my M.Tech results and to join the spicy delicious lunch. I chose the PC as I had workedfor a year to see this day. It was the day for which God only knows how much my mother bribed him for, since I was a small kid, and today she is doing the same with a greater magnitude for my results. I find my mind abducted in storms when I start contemplating the contribution of God and those bribes in my degree.

Chuck it... It's high time to concentrate on the entrance results. This was the last thing I was doing for mom.

I could find the server as down as my blown off mind.

Result out. Roll no.... I could see my mom was struggling to close her eyes and go in her hypothetical world of Gods where she could ask them a little, but she was forced to peep and find what happened with my results.

My heart beat skipped, it almost stopped, everything in front of me was turning black, I could feel the difference between my heartbeat and my breath.

Ayaan Dixit- PASS

Mom hugged me, I reestablished my senses.

Yes, my computer became my best friend, my room, my chair, everything seemed so lucky to me or may be the presence of the most beautiful lady, whose shivering hands were throughout on my shoulder. That hot sunny day soon became a pleasant one for me and mom. I knew mom was unable to express her feeling. It was more than a dream come true for my mom. I was living it because she was happy.

Soon evening things changed, perception for my tomorrow changed. Mom was required to break all the fix deposits to collect the funds required for my further studies which she has been saving for so long. They were fifteen difficult days that I has passed with mom, keeping in mind that I was leaving her soon.

Finally that difficult day arrived when I was supposed to go to college. Saying that 'Bye' to mom, was difficult. Her delicate expression made me emotional. I knew it was difficult for her to live without me, to live all alone. But I was doing this for her. She always wanted me to do this. And that lonesome train whistle, most bothersome sound so far, that was an indication of me and mom's separation. It seemed like my new life was calling me, but I was heartbroken, tensed and things appeared so still to me. This was going to be one difficult journey.

I was few minutes away from my destination. And suddenly something happened.

A voice… No No No… Not just a voice. Someone's voice more melodious than a nightingale. That laugh, OMG

I struggled hard to get a mere glimpse of her. Long hair tie up in a pony, ankle-touching multicolored skirt, a funky top, a single silver metal thin bangle, and colorful Rajasthani foot wear. I tried to think of a word to describe her, but I could not think, I could not blink. I was just in awe. I wanted her to look at me. I wanted to get a glimpse of her face. Somehow, I already felt connected to her.

Oh yes my bloody destiny leaves no chance of proving itself. I reached Delhi before I could see her. Puke on me, my luck, and my life. I went out, got into a *rickshaw* and asked him to take me to my hostel address. I spoke to mom over the phone, had dinner and laid in bed staring at the ceiling, I wanted to think of mom, my next day in college and my future but what came to my mind, ears and moreover my heart was that melodious voice. I was already in love with that someone whom I saw in the train.

Next day I went to college, the campus was huge. After having struggled to find my classroom I went in and waited as I was early. So there were yet 20 min remaining for class to begin. 20 minutes passed like 20 seconds and I was still thinking of the same girl. The professor entered and things turned serious. I was sitting alone, may be because my appearance justifies me a perfect 'BORING PERSON' and none of them wanted to get bored sitting beside me.

Just as the lecture was about to begin I heard a voice: "Could I come in sir?" The very same voice I had been thinking about. I looked up and saw her, her eyes... ah... breathtaking.

Professor allowed her to enter the class. While at one hand my fondness for her was getting desperate with every next blink of her, I on the other, was still waiting for her to notice me. Like destiny would have it, she could not find any seat and sat next to me.

I could not control myself and asked her "Are you the same girl who was in the train yesterday?"

"Do you want me and yourself to get out of this class? Shut up and look in front."

My naughty brain thought "That's exactly what I want."

But the class came to an end, much to my disappointment.

She said "So... Hi!"

OMG, she is talking to me. I thought to myself, how desperate I was in the matter of mirco-seconds.

She repeated "Hello?"

Something, that I would later reflect upon as embarrassment, made me say the words I said next: "I hate your eyes"

She said "What?"

"I hate loving things."

"What's wrong with you?"

She picked up her bag suddenly, and began walking out. But just then she turned a little and smiled at me. I felt that was enough to kill me. I did a little salsa holding her hand in my head. For me the Day ended well. Just as I lay in the bed for the night, I though, *I just wanted her to wish me "Good night" because without this my night would not go good. But expectations leads to disappointment. I assumed she wished me, without letting me know.*

The next day we became FRIENDS. Yes... yes we did. And it was she who proposed the idea.

We were together, complete and happy now. We used to text each other on holidays the entire day. I wanted to see her every time when I could not. Her smile was my breakfast, her laughter were the reason my heart beated, those winks were like dessert. I was in love with her. I loved the way she looked at me. I loved the way how she counted in hindi 'ek, do, teen..... pacchis, chhabis, twenty seven, twenty eight, twenty nine...'

I loved the way she sung the same song exclusively for me every time.

I loved the way she chose golgappa over pizza.

I loved the way she chewed the back of my pencil.

I loved the way she talked like a kid.

I loved the way she called my name so cutely in between her laughter.

I loved each and everything about her.

Results for the first semester were out. I went to the notice board alone as I was a bit early to college. We both scored well. I was searching for Kashish. I was searching everywhere for her and then I saw Kashish with a guy. They both were hugging each other. I went close to them, though I wanted to go away from them. Kashish was saying to this guy "I missed you Sid."

Sid replied by hugging her "Oh my sweet heart... I love you."

I stood frozen, my eyes were red when Kasish saw me and said "Oh Ayaan come here... look who is here. This is Sid my childhood friend."

Sid said laughingly "And this is my sweet heart, my future girl and your friend Kashish. I love her so much"

They both laughed, my surrounding laughed, I felt like everything was laughing on me. We had a little interaction and I left them.

I went straight to my hostel. Switched off the lights and jumped in bed. I tried hard to sleep but just could not. Things had appeared so ugly to me. I was pissed off. This girl who meant everything to me loved some other guy. I was just a so called FRIEND to her. I did not go to college for the next three days. I switched off my cell phone. Someone informed me that Kashish came to the hostel to check whether everything was okay or not. My friends informed her that I was not in town.

After knowing this I went to college the next day and found Kashish sitting on our favorite bench in the garden area. It was damn difficult for me to face her but in any way I was forced to do so. I went to her. Her head was bent down. I called her name. She looked at me and I saw tears in her eyes. Her voice choked, she wanted to take my name but she could not. I could not resist myself to go away from her, I thought she needed me. She needed a shoulder to cry on and she hugged me. I Her tears touched my cheeks. Ah... I felt so much pain as if someone has put a knife through my heart, it was piercing deep inside, breaking ribs and all I could do was watch

I regained my courage and said "Calm down Kashu... what happened?"

"My parents want me to get married and they are super serious this time."

This was another shock for me. I wiped off tears and said, "Okay do not cry, we will discuss this."

"No... No... I can't live with it, we need to discuss it now. Stop being so carefree everytime." Kashish shouted.

"Okay so what is the problem?"

"I don't want to get married and the guy is the main problem."

"To whom do they want you to marry?"

"It's Sid."

My name must get registered in Guinness Book for surviving so many shocks. Kashish loves Sid, Sid loves Kashish, Kashish's family loves Sid then what the hell is problem?

"So...?" I said.

"So... What? I don't want to marry Sid."

"You love him. Right?"

"Yes I do... he is my friend damn it."

I wanted to dance. I wanted to sing. I wanted to do every freaking thing after listening that.

She continued "Sid is a rich guy, we are childhood friends. Dad always wanted me to be with a man like Sid. Biggest problem is that Sid wants to marry me."

This was the first time I did not have any problem with tears in her eyes.

"Okay stop it now. He is your friend, I am your friend. What the hell do you want actually?"

Her expression changed, the pitch of her voice changed.

She said "I don't know what is happening. I am confused, things are different. Life has never been as wonderful to me as it is been for last one and half year. I feel so much complete now. I know we are friends but believe me our relationship is better than any other relation. I have no idea whether it is the saddest thing or the luckiest thing when we both really know each other. Our secrets, our fears, our favorite things. We have learned how to calm each other, how to tame each other's demon and now back to strangers, can't walk past and pretend like we never knew each other. Last three days were the most difficult days for me. Damn it Ayaan."

She was literally shouting this time.

And then I kissed her, our lips enveloped. Thirty seconds passed and that life giving moment.

I said "I Love You, I love you more than anything, just be mine please."

A fifteen minutes tight hug. It was not the first time we hugged each other. But that feel was out of this world.

"Ayaan… I Love You too. But things are difficult. My dad will never accept you.'

"Why? Doesn't he like monkeys?"

"Ah… Shut up. See 'I love you' is just the beginning. He wants a rich guy, a really rich guy, we are also not from the same caste."

I was on my on my kneeI said *"Well in that case we will face this. Look Kashu I have never been so serious in my life as I am now. Let the situation try its best, we'll still be together, forever. I can fight with the whole world for you, all I want is your hand in mine, doesn't matter if I lose, I'll fight, just to let the world know about our bond, how strong it is. We can survive the storm, as long as we are together. I can cross any heights or boundaries just to bring this beautiful curve on your face. You look gorgeous with this smile. I will sing for you, I will dance for you just to make you forget all the pains you have ever been through. Yeah I will do because I am your man. We have been through a lot, still we are holding on to each other. You know what makes us stay together? Our belief and trust in each other. Does not matter if you start hating me. I will love you with double the intensity. Does not matter if you give up on me, I will come back to you, with double the trust. I promise you I will never cause any hurt to you."*

When I looked up she had tears in her eyes.

I resisted my tears and gathered strength to say "Your smile acts like a powerhouse to me…"

I pretended that I am strong enough not to cry. There was a permanent real smile on my face.

She said "Stop please…," and kissed me.

I said "Now what next?"

She smiled and said "Let's love each other and convince our parents."

"Okay then, I am coming to meet your dad tomorrow."

"Tomorrow? Won't that be early?"

"Nah, because I can't afford being late."

"Hmm… Okay."

We kissed each other and said bye. Before leaving Kashish asked me, "What if he doesn't agrees?"

"We will still fight for our love. Loving someone from the bottom of heart is not easy as it seems. People have to face destiny. Some kneel down in front of it and we will make even destiny bow its head in front of them."

When she left, she was smiling.

I didn't slept the entire night in tension. Next day Kashish wished me luck and I went to her house. Till then Kashish had already convinced her parents to meet me at least for once. I reached there. It was a huge house. I can say this was the biggest bungalow I had seen in reality.

The watchman took me to them. I saw Kashish, I wanted to hug her but we both were not in condition to do so. I was literally shivering, and I broke a sweat. Her father asked me some general questions where I was good at. I could see Kashish was praying in her mind for things to go well. And then something unexpected happened.

Her dad suddenly said "We don't have any problem."

Kashish and I stood up, unable to believe this was really happening.

He said "I love my daughter, and she loves you. I have enough of money for her. If she finds her happiness in you, I will be the happiest dad if she gets you."

Kashish came running to her dad and hugged him thanking him. Everything went freaking well. Next day I was out for some work when I received a message from Kashish's dad on my cell phone texting, "We need to meet NOW. Come to my office."

I was nervous. I didn't tell Kashish about the text. Our conversation started normally, it was in gentle flow until he said, "LEAVE MY DAUGHTER, You have no idea what you have messed up. It's Raviraj Arora this time. I love my reputation and fame. I love my image and if for this I will have to pay my daughter as cost I will do that too. I will kill you. I won't mind killing my daughter if it is to safeguard my reputation. No one can ruin it. Siddharth is the perfect guy for her. Look at yourself... where do you stand in front of me? I can hire thousands of employees with your degree in the same office where you are standing right now. You don't have anyl family background. What if my colleagues ask me about my son-in-law? What is your market value? Just nothing. Do you have any idea what

Siddharth can provide her? You will ruin her life. She deserves much better than you. Enough of giving lecture. I have not called you here to convince you. Look… I already have marriage cards printed for Kashish and SIddharth. This first one is for you. Fifth day from now is the final marriage day as I can't take any risk now. Either convince her for marriage or get ready for her funeral on sixth day.

I went out of his office. What was this happening with me? And why me? I COULD NOT LET anything happen to Kashish. I convinced myself in thoughts, that her dad was right in a way. Siddharth is a nice and compatible guy for Kashish. He is gentle. He is rich and I am nothing more than shit for Kashish. She deserves him.

I messaged Kashish "Look Shivani… I Love You. Kashish is just a game. A game for some time. She is rich and I need money. She is a stupid girl, who believes me blindly. It's a planned marriage. Her dad's position in the market will let me achieve high. Just two years won't change my mind. I have to be with her only for the next six months. I LOVE YOU SWEET HEART."

Kashish called me multiple number of times but I did not receive her call. She came to my hostel hurriedly and showed me the same message on her cell phone.

She said "Speak up moron."

"Kashu… this is fake.'

"What's fake? This message? You? Or your love?"

"Okay Kashish believe me I will leave her. I Love You. I will leave her. She was in my last college. She is my friend."

"F-R-I-E-N-D?" she said

"I am sorry Kashish, this won't happen again"

"S-O-R-R-Y, F-R-I-E-N-D, I believed you. I Loved you."

She slapped me many times and left the hostel. She was heartbroken.

That day, I realized much later, I made the worst thing in my life. I made her cry.

AND SHE HATES ME NOW.

Four days later, one of my friends informed me about distribution of Kashish's and Siddharth's marriage card. Soon, the day of her marriage rolled in. *I was pretending that I was strong. But I am was crying in an empty room and writing this, I don't want to know the sorcery to hide my tears now. I know I understand her. I can stand behind her. Most annoying fact is I can understand the pain she is facing right now BECAUSE OF ME. I can feel my soul leaving my body. Her dad made me feel worthless even though Kashish deserves my true love. I know she must be so broken deep inside. I can't figure out Kashish's sadness. Is it me or my love?*

All I know is I LOVE HER, I LOVE HER and I LOVE HER. I CAN'T LIVE WITHOUT HER.

Kashish closed the diary, shocked beyond words, beyond tears.

I still remembered that day.

She always knew Ayaan loved herand could never cheat on her. Sheagreed to marry Sid only to provoke Ayaan to confess Even Sid was a part of the plan. So she waited for Ayaan till the last moment of the marriage ceremony to begin. She was sure he would come. But when he did not come, she ran from the house, to his hostel in her bridal dress.

There she found his body hanging from the ceiling fan.

She found this diary lying on the ground close to him. For others, he killed himself. But for her he had given up his life.

It's been five years now that Ayaan is no more. Kashish teaches in the same college where they had studied together. She finds solace in the surroundings that remind her of him. She is no more in contact with the man who was the reason Ayaan had been tricked in the first place. Her father. Ayaan's mom lives with me. She is happy, or may be pretends to be so. It's easy to think about past, but it's painful to get into the same past where you have lived and felt so many things. Ahh… Ayaan… my world! My life!

Life would be completely different if Ayaan had been here but I still don't regret anything because I know Ayaan wants me to be happy.

I remember the time when I could not imagine living without him And see now I am living without him, surviving for so long.

Dates changed, months changed and Kashish is there, with a little hope, passing each day.

"Ayaan you were right… our LOVE won… we are still together, it's just that we are not with each other. But I can always feel you and I know you see me every time from wherever you are. Destiny bowed its head for OUR LOVE."

He is not dead, nor am I. We both are alive.
I LIVE FOR HIM,
HE LIVES IN ME.

"Tujhe chaand tha pasand, Aaj tu chaand ke bagal wala tara hai

Kabhi yaha tha, Aaj aasmaan me bhi aashiyaan humara hai

Tu dar mat, Nahi aarahi ye duniya chodke main tere paas

Jism se nahi, Khuda ne rooh se bnaya humara saath hai"

Akash Shrivastav

Mumbai based Akash Shrivastav is currently pursuing CA. He has contributed short stories to few anthologies like - It's All About You, Myriad Tales, Secrets of Soul and Zest of Inklings. He has also contributed articles to a couple of e-magazines, namely Blending Mind and Intellinotions.

He likes reading suspense and thriller stories. He is also passionate about music – trance, EDMs, pop, dub-steps etc. and boxing. He likes hanging out and partying with friends.

You can reach him at -https://www.facebook.com/himalay.shrivastav.1

Ashwati Menon

Ashwati Menon, a Kerala*ite*, born brought up in Gujarat began writing since she was 8 years old. The journey began with short poems, followed by short stories and novel. She published her debut novel 'Let Me Sleep!' under the pen name, Anita Raghav. She has also contributed a short story to the anthology, Secrets of Soul. She is currently working in an IT Software Company as a Project Manager. Her hobbies include reading, dancing and playing guitar.

You can reach her at - https://www.facebook.com/ashwati.menon?fref=ts

13

THE SECOND PHASE-
LOVE THAT LETS YOU LIVE

Akash Srivastav & Ashwati Menon

"And I vow that I will always keep Niharika happy…."
"I will love her a lot!!" saying this Dev took seven rounds of trust, bonding and love before the holy fire holding Niharika's hand.

*****

Dev Banerjee, a successful lawyer and one of the richest eligible bachelors in India married Niharika Sharma on 15th November, 2007. He had an attractive personality and perfect physique which was worth dying for. But he didn't have something that he would have really lived for – or for that matter someone to really love for. Niharika was perhaps that one reason he really hung on to life.

Having lost his parents in India, Dev had never really had a chance to get over the shock of their bodies not being recovered. What was visible of them were their ring fingers. *Perhaps that is the power of love*, Dev had thought as he had lighted the pyre. He had flown back from United States where he had been living with his uncle and first cousins.

The marriage ceremony went with great pomp and show. It was one of the most attractive marriage ceremonies anyone could have ever imagined and the local media was covering it like some kind of great (choice of a better word) to be enjoyed and eaten.

Standing in the corner of a room, overlooking the balcony, clad in full bridal clothes, was Niharika. In her hand she clutched a piece of paper. It was a lost brick from the walls of time. She knew the contents of the piece of paper. She knew what that paper said. But she didn't have the guts to read it again. Reading it again would only make her relived the pain that she had tried to suppress all these years.

Nevertheless, she opened the paper and saw in it, written right across the page with funny and silly smileys: *Niharika, you have a funny button nose and you should rent it to this hotel manager to put on his coat!*

Niharika smiled silently. She remembered the fateful day she had gone to lunch before it all had happened and how *he* had made fun of her nose and made fun of the Hotel Manager too. Nothing sinister – just fun. Niharika had laughed until her jaws had ached.

Niharika was not at all happy with this marriage. Again she remembered *his* words: *Sometimes making others happy gives us all the happiness in the world.* She could see in the distance how the groom was easily perched on the mare and everyone around him were bouncing off the streets. Indian marriages never lose class. She wanted to run away from this marriage. But she wanted to stay, for Dev.

"I am sorry Prathamesh!!" she silently murmured herself, "I love you and I will live for you!"

Tears ran down her eyes and faded on her cheeks. *If there is ever going to be a next life Prathamesh, I will be there with you. If I cannot be, I will come with you to meet our creator. I will live this life like a dead soul – I will live for you and our dreams. I will live thinking of you every minute of my life.*

Niharika was a simple, beautiful girl of 27 years and very down to earth. Innocent, childish by nature, she had bubbly looks with a chubby face and cute hazel eyes. Her hair was long like that of Rapunzel in the fairy tale. She was the obvious first choice of all the men around her. The only thing was that nobody perhaps knew her first choice.

****

The marriage ceremony was successful and everyone had returned to their respective homes. Niharika went with Dev to his house. This was going to be her home for the rest of her life – this was the paradise, this was her hell, this was everything.

The in-laws home is what every girl desires for, something every girl has been taught to dream about.

The next morning, Dev woke up happily greeting his newly wedded wife. But Niharika didn't pay any heed to his words and went to the kitchen for preparing the breakfast. Meanwhile, her phone rang.

"I'm coming in 30 minutes"; she replied and prepared the breakfast hurriedly.

"Ahmm, Niha, Sorry, Niharika?' edged Dev to the entrance of the kitchen. Niharika nodded from her rolling pin but didn't look up.

Dev continued fidgeting with the wall, "Look, we are now a married couple. Let's go out for the whole day and in the evening we can go to the beach," Dev said sheepishly and continued further, "I heard that you love to visit beaches."

"Thank you Dev! But, I have to meet someone today and it's very important for me. I will come home in the evening." Niharika replied, as she bolted at a fast pace.

"Okay," Dev replied.

Niharika left the house and a disappointed Dev went to his office. In the evening, Dev returned home but there was no trace of Niharika. After 3 hours, she returned home.

"Hey darling, where were you?" Dev asked worriedly, trying hard at a conversation starter.

"I was in the meeting and don't worry I had my dinner. I had prepared yours. I will get it hot for you and then I will sleep. I am bone-tired." saying this Niharika went to sleep.

Dev was taken aback. He was getting paranoid thinking of the whole thing. *What's wrong with her! What was the whole point of this marriage – I am still having lonely dinners.*

Dev bit his lip and pushed away the plate and went to the garden – *Come on God! Tell me what else am I supposed to lose? My peace of mind!*

****

For Dev, the marriage was slowly turning into a failed attempt at having a resurrected normal life. One bad incident had torn his world into pieces – the Mumbai floods of 2005 that had ripped the State of Maharashtra to pieces and Dev's life too; the other event had been his marriage. For him it was a brave effort to even think of settling down with a woman – losing parents had never gotten over his conscious mind.

But Niharika's absolute aloof behavior was gnawing at a part of him. It hadonly been a day, he accepted and he had to give enough room to an average Indian girl to get over her coyness. But here, she seemed to be avoiding him outright.

Is Niharika not happy with the marriage? Was she forced into accepting me? Or is there someone else with whom she had the "meeting"!

Dev was trying to straighten his thoughts but nothing made sense whatsoever. He was worried that he might lose her forever too.

When he had first seen her picture, he was really not interested. But then when he repeatedly saw it, he could see the melancholy beauty that she was and it was the hollow pain in her eyes that won him over. It was a solace that he found, as if someone knew him much better.

The next morning, Dev got ready for his office and before leaving the office he told Niharika, "Niharika, I have booked 2 passes for Rahat Fateh Ali Khan's concert. I want you to accompany me for the show. Please make yourself free in the evening."

"Okay. I will remember," she replied with a smile. Dev was surprised to see it.

The concert was a big success for the artist and Dev too. Rahat Fateh Ali Khan's entire fan-flock were moving to his romantic numbers as though led by some pied piper.

Meanwhile, the most favorite romantic song was being sung by Rahat Fateh Ali Khan;

*Main tenu samjhawan ki.. Na tere bina lagda jee…*It was the favorite romantic song going on the charts so far and people screamed their throats out when the first soulful tunes started floating off the stage.

"I Love You Niharika!!" saying this Dev held her hand and kissed it.

She withdrew her hand immediately, and said, "I'm not feeling well Dev. Shall we go home please?"

"Okay," replied Dev, fearing that this disappointment was never ending. Every attempt to normalize things was going out of hands and he was constantly struggling to improvise.

Niharika was lost in her thoughts. She had travelled many years back in life when there was somebody else who used to rule her thoughts. She knew that time was not coming back – Prathamesh was not coming back. She wanted to shout. She wanted to scream and wanted to cry like a small baby, but she couldn't. Only silent tears rolled down her eyes.

"Niharika, are you okay?" asked Dev while driving the car, "What's wrong?"

"Nothing," she replied and wiped her tears, "I am fine."

Dev and Niharika reached home and retired to their bed. Dev couldn't sleep that night, disturbed and worried, he e was puzzled with Niharika's behavior.

"Have I done something wrong? Why doesn't she love me? These questions were constantly running in his mind.

Dev knew hated this loneliness. He despised the idea but he knew he had to go through Niharika's things. He could not be in this limbo state forever. He wanted answers as to what happened and why they were happening this way, why things were being this difficult with Niharika.

So the next day, when Niharika had left for an "urgent meeting"; he opened her wardrobe and went through some stuffs – all were clothes and accessories. Buried deep in a corner of the cupboard was a pink folder and a diary that was trying to hide itself beneath a shirt but was somehow peeping out. Dev grabbed it and went to his room.

So this is where you have kept yourself Niharika, thought Dev.

It was a very huge folder and he could see many love letters written in hearts, kisses and hugs. Dev understood one thing for sure; Niharika had a past love life and she had concealed it beneath this marriage.

He then closed the folders and opened her diary to read it. It was decorated with the stickers of hearts, roses and cupids.

****

12th January, 2003

Being a junior accountant of my company, I was called upon in a meeting to assist my seniors in discussing the company's financial statements and their growth status. It was a boring day for me; after all it was a Sunday – one of my favorite days where I would lie on my bed like a dead log till late afternoon. The sickening Debits and Credit balances is creating a hole in my brain.

But alas! I was in my company attending the meeting.

Destiny had stored something else for me. Maybe, the cupid- God of love, was ready to pierce the arrow of love in my body.

I happened to see a guy in the meeting. He was quite cute and handsome as well. He was a chocolate boy…Oh, he was so cute!!

The meeting ended in a few hours, but during the lunch time, he was nowhere to be seen.

And thus, my day ended imagining his cute face with a sweet smile.

In a jiffy, I fell for him. It was 'LOVE AT FIRST SIGHT!

13th January, 2003

It was Monday. Yawn!!

As usual, I was suffering from Monday blues. Somehow, I got ready and reached office.

And I happened to see him! My charming prince again in the office! I was very happy. My heart was singing.

Through my friends, I came to know that he was new to our office. Oh my God! I wanted to talk to him. I wanted to be with him.

I wish I could have extended my hand for friendship.

But, I was scared of rejection.

Thus, my day ended in deciding whether I should take the first step or not. This is such a sick feeling Diary, you have no clue. I am happy you don't have to fall in love.

20th February, 2003

My dear diary!! Today I am very happy.

Today my company approached me and my charming prince and were told to accompany along with our team members for a business exhibition at Kolkata.

I was very happy on hearing this. My charming prince was going to accompany me. I was on cloud nine.

Diary!! My sweetie, I want to express what I feel for him.

He is so sweet, so polite and handsome; Prince Charming of my dreams.

23rd February, 2003

Dear Diary,

It was a fruitful day.. We both spoke to each other for the first time and got introduced to each other. He was impressed by my performance and couldn't stop himself from praising me.

All I could do was to look into his eyes. I was totally lost in him.

<u>When Love truly rings:</u>

The irritating meeting, the untimely entry, the business trip and our friendship – seems so ethereal and out of this world. I don't remember when God made men like him but glad that he preserved one for me.

****

Dev unfurled the pages of her diary.

The diary was filled with the memories of their friendship.

After sometime, he came upon a page where she had expressed her happiness.

****

25th December, 2003

Ho Ho Ho!!
Merry Christmas Diary…..

You know, today Prathamesh proposed to me.
He took me for a ride in a hot air balloon. Soon, he bowed on his knees and proposed.
Without wasting a second, I said Yes!
It was the best gift of my life.
Thank you Santa!! Thank you for listening and answering my prayers…

****

Dev was enraged after reading this.

Niharika loves Prathamesh, then why did she agree to marry me?
Why did she vow for the relation of trust and honesty before the holy fire?"

Dev said to himself and punched his fist on the wall.

"I will divorce Niharika. I don't want to be with someone the love that is not mine! She loves Prathamesh."

Saying this, he flung the diary towards the wall.

As the diary fell down on the ground, he saw a sketch of a sad girl. She was weeping.

Dev found it strange and then picked up the diary and began reading again.

****

RAIN!!!!

I love rain a lot!!

It brings happiness and a big smile on our face. The weather becomes quite romantic. The smell of the fresh mud... Ah!!

It really rejuvenates us.

But, I never ever thought in my life that this rain which I love a lot would take away my happiness. My life!!

26ᵗʰ July, 2005

It was raining a lot since 25ᵗʰ June.

Monsoon seemed to not taking a break at all. It was raining heavily.

Prathamesh and I had decided to go to Juhu beach at evening to see the high tide waves so that we would stand there watching the water and talking, eating hot pakoras – oh yes! Not to forget the hot tea that we had decided to have. The idea is yummy! (I loved the damn pakoras!)

It was 11.30 am. I rang Prathamesh and he told me that he would come to my place at afternoon as he had a surprise for me. I was very excited and was also very eager to know it.

At around 2pm, he called me and told that he was near Pawai and would be coming at my house to discuss regarding our marriage to my parents. I was very glad on hearing this.

It was like I was on cloud nine.

I waited for him. But he didn't come. I rang him, but his cell phone was untraceable.

At evening, Prathamesh's mother had called me to ask me if he had come at my house or not. She was very worried.

But unfortunately, I came through news channels that Pawai area was heavily flooded due to rain and there was also a cloudburst. Many people were carried away by the strong flow of water.

Without thinking for a second, I found myself leaving the house in search of Prathamesh. But Dad stopped me and assured me that they would begin the search operation for Prathamesh the next day, as it was late night.

I was worried the whole night. I couldn't lie still for a single second.

All I wanted was to see Prathamesh who used to hold me and melt me in his arms. Whenever I looked at him, I used to completely forget the world.

27ᵗʰ July, 2005

Day dawned, but there was no sunlight. The sky was covered with dark black clouds.

It was raining cats and dogs.

Dad and I went to search Prathamesh at Pawai, but that area was heavily flooded. There was water everywhere. It seemed as if the Tsunami had paid a visit to our city.

We came home empty-handed.

Soon my phone rang and I got news. It changed my life forever.

His friend had informed that Prathamesh's car got stuck near a water logged area and got drifted away. He seemed to have gone away with the strong currents of water.

I fainted on hearing this.

Later when I regained my consciousness, I found myself on the hospital bed.

I was informed that PRATHAMESH WAS NO MORE!!

His body was recovered from the flood water and was badly swollen.

I was broken from inside.......

I couldn't believe that PRATHAMESH WAS NO MORE!!

My World!! My Life!!

Everything was snatched by destiny................

Prathamesh, why did you go! Please come back!

I can't live without you...

Come back!!!!

*****

Dev stood rooted to his spot. He could not believe what he was reading. There was another chapter.

He hurriedly went through more of the written content and came to the last part of the folder. A photograph of Prathamesh and Niharika; actually there were many and so he saw all of them. But the first one was a whiplash.

He could not get over his thoughts: *Prathamesh Sahni, you were Niharika's first love? You are the one who is governing her thoughts? Prathamesh, have you really left all of us and gone?*

He felt terrible. For Dev, it was like gulping acid. Prathamesh and Dev had been together in college. Prathamesh had proceeded to continue his masters while Dev had gone to United States to complete his higher studies. The once good chums drifted apart as Dev got lost in his new life in U.S. and Prathamesh busied himself in completing masters. He could not believe that the once happy – go – lucky Prathamesh was no more in the world.

Dev got up and wiped his tears.

"Hi Dev!" a voice echoed the room.

Dev looked at the direction of the voice and was shocked to see a guy standing there.

That guy was none other than Prathamesh- Niharika's *first love*. He knew it was an apparition; something his mind had conjured up.

"Prathamesh! You are here", said Dev shockingly.

"Yes Dev," nodded back the figure, "We were friends in college; I know you remember."

Dev was shocked to know how his mind had conjured up Prathamesh.

Prathamesh continued,"You know Dev we were both fools that we lost ourselves in the new life. We never even bothered to call back or contact each other. We never realize what we have until we lose it. I know it will be tough for you to accept Niharika's love life with me, but trust me - she would be the one woman with whom you might want to grow old."

Dev looked silently at Prathamesh.

"Yes. These are difficult times. But nothing emerges victorious, not even a mighty emperor of any country, without trying and slogging through tough times. Dev, an entire lifetime passes and people still never love their partners. They keep brooding their whole life – they even have kids but there is always a void that cannot be filled. Don't make this mess out of your life. Talk to her about me – she wants to be understood and she will understand, once you speak to her."

"You think she will?" asked Dev.

"Yes Dev, I have seen the true love in your eyes and I also know that you love her a lot! I request you to accept her in your life.

She needs your love. Please don't leave her!"

Dev couldn't fight back his tears.

Prathamesh held his hand, "Dev, promise me! Promise me that you will love Niharika a lot. You won't make her realize my absence. PROMISE ME DEV!"

With that he vanished! Dev's apparition ended. He blinked and saw the living room of his house come into focus.

That eveningthe scene unfolded like that of a movie. Niharika was standing near the staircase holding to the wooden railing and Dev was sitting at the dining table. He held in his hand Niharika's diary and was sobbing into his sleeve. The final confrontation was over. Dev couldn't believe it.

"But why is it affecting you so much Dev?" said Niharika, perplexed and confused.

"Because I not only lost my parents but my friend Prathamesh too in those floods Niharika –your first love. Your first love was my friend in college. He was my close friend and we lost contact after I moved to United States. I never knew I had lost him too."

Niharika did not wait. She got up and went over to him. She hugged him tightly then as Dev sobbed into her shoulders. Niharika could feel her own eyes fill-up.

"Niharika, I love you a lot! My life starts with you and ends with you! You complete me Niharika!" saying this Dev kissed Niharika on her forehead.

Niharika, only hugged him tighter.

They didn't eat food that night. It was more for both than they could take. Niharika checked her mobile phone – it was 3 AM and she decided she could sleep no more. There was no point in trying so hard to sleep. She knew what day it was and she had some little work to do.

This twisted and toxic thing is over. Dev, it's time to start our story...

*****

After a few hours, the morning dawned with a musical tone of 'Happy Birthday!'

Dev opened his eyes and was surprised to see Niharika greeting him.

She had a sweet smile on her face which surely fitted the phrase 'A MILLION DOLLAR SMILE'.

"Thank you so much honey!" Dev jumped in joy and continued further,

"But how is that you know my birthday?"

"I went through your stuffs and pestered your cousins; they told me. I didn't let them sleep either." she smiled and offered him a cup of tea.

Dev was surprised with the sudden change in Niharika's behavior, but welcomed this new verison of hers. He held her hand and pulled her towards him and asked mischievously,"Hey, today is my Birthday. Won't you make it special?"

"In what sense?" she asked with a smile that had mirrored the mischief.

"Let's go somewhere today evening where it's just us and the open air."

He brought her closer – close enough to feel her breath. Niharika closed her eyes. Dev touched her lips with his lips.

He kissed her to his heart's content.

It reminded him of lines by Robert Burns:

Humid seal of soft affections,
Tend 'rest pledge of future bliss,
Dearest tie of young connections,
Love's first snow-drop, virgin kiss.
Speaking silence, dumb confession,
Passion's birth, and infants' play,
Dove-like fondness, chaste concession,
Glowing dawn of brighter day.
Sorrowing joy, adieu's last action,
Ling'ring lips, -- no more to join!
What words can ever speak affection
Thrilling and sincere as thine!

*****

The next day, Dev got ready and left hurriedly

An hour later, his car honked at the gate and Niharika went to the gate.

She was surprised to see Prathamesh's mother standing with Dev.

"Ma!" Niharika exclaimed in joy and ran towards her. She hugged her in joy.

"Niharika, from today onwards Maa will stay with us. I called from your cell phone – sorry for that – but then I came to know that you used to visit Ma in the ashram under the pretext of going to office. You don't have to that anymore, Ma will stay with us here." Dev said with a smile on his face.

Niharika smiled and thanked him with joy as they made their way inside the house.

Both were thinking the same thing. Both were thanking God for the new beginning.

Ketaki Sane

Rightly known as 'an author with the right mix of intelligence & compassion', for her debut work -Romantic Resonance, Mumbai based Ketaki Sane believes in following her heart. She has written a couple of short stories too along with articles in e-magazines.

Shefirmly believes that, 'good things happen by chance', just like writing happened to her! She wants her writing to inspire others just like the writings of great people inspire her.

You can reach her at -https://www.facebook.com/ketakis15

14

THAT'S THE SPIRIT!

Ketaki Sane

Prologue

Memories are mad, simply mad! They trap you up irrespective of being good or bad! If good, they make you nostalgic and if bad they make you shudder, but both trap you in a time frame. Sometimes our dreams are drawn from memories, memories hidden under layers of grey matter, beneath the seat of the sub-conscious mind, with its roots extended even beyond this life. In case of some unfortunate individuals, the door that separates this life and the life beyond, remains open, leading to superimposed memories.

I would have never believed this could happen even in today's times, as if I had been the third person in the whole scenario. Only because I was a witness and also a victim, I have agreed to narrate my story. It will be published in the all India magazine named, 'Anhoone' meaning *strange*.

The Story

Life wasn't exactly a bed of roses even before I could hear *his* voice. I was an outcast in my family, a good-for-nothing fellow; and so if they ever find about this, they would tag me 'mad.' My father spoke to me with disgrace, I loathed my brother and my mother never have a say in anything. *His* laughter had sent a shiver down my spine. I had entered the phase of self-pitying. Things changed drastically for me, when I finally confronted him.

I was leading a perfect-loser-life any college going student does. I looked decent and the small white scar on the jaw made me look cute, at least that was what girls said! My name and looks were both similar to Sushant Singh, the Kai Po Che actor, that was the only plus point. I wasn't the rich and smart types so I could not woo girls like the *richies* did, but the day Suhana spoke to me, people started noticing me. Later as it turned out, she had only spoken to me as part of a dare. Her boyfriend had challenged her to speak to any random guy and ask for a lift. I usually commuted to college by bus, but luckily that day, I had my brother's bike which he had offered to me, only because he wanted meto fill petrol.

She came up to me with a standard, 'Excuse me?'

Although I did hear a female voice, I didn't bother to turn around assuming it was not for me.

'Excuse me?' she repeated and then I turned around questioningly, 'Me?'

'Can you please drop me to the station?' she asked plainly without making eye contact.

'What, me, but, but you travel by car…I don't have one…' I said confused. I had obviously noticed her several times and knew few things about her.

Maybe I saw a hint of surprise on her plain face. 'Well yes, but today…the driver is on leave.'

'Umm, are you sure you want to go with me on my bike?' I confirmed and scanned the area to check how many people were noticing. I was obviously happy.

'Yes. Station.' She smiled or maybe it was my imagination.

I hardly realized her weight as she sat on the bike, but yes, her perfume made up for it. The station was a ten minute drive and my heart was racing faster than the bike.

'Thank you.' She got down and spoke softly.

'Yaa, no problem' I was about to say, but she ran off to a car standing nearby and I saw a group of rich asses laughing their stomach out, pointing at her and then at me! I kind of guessed what the whole thing was and well I couldn't do more than feel bad about it.

Suhana was obviously better off without me.

I was playing the scene in my mind as I climbed the stairs of the dingy chawl where I lived. The door opened before I could even knock on it and there sat my father with his arms folded, signaling interrogation, just as my mother hurried to the kitchen. I put the bike keys in the drawer which I would never have done normally, had that Hitler not been there. I don't know why but I was very much scared of my father!

'Your brother and I earn money for your education and you spend it on girls.' he roared, not flexing those taut muscles an inch!

My bad! Why did he have to see me the only time I was with a girl, that too dropping her off as a part of some stupid ploy! Explaining the reality would not make any sense, he wouldn't believe, so I cooked up some lame story that she was a classmate and a goon was troubling her so she asked me to drop her to station. His expression changed, he was starting to unfold his arms too, but I didn't wait longer than this, to check whether he was convinced or not. I ran out of the house to meet my chawl-buddies.

Incidentally, one of them had also seen me drop Suhana and I was the hero of the day. We chatted, gossiped (yes, even guys gossip), shared our respective days, dreamed about being someone someday, about contributing to this society and what not. Yes, we also discussed and rated girls – all shapes and sizes that passed our sight. It was getting dark and my stomach was rumbling. I so much wanted to hog on roti-sabzi but without my father's tadka. I spotted my elder brother entering the lane, his hands were occupied with vegetables for the week. I knew this was my turn to enter the house without being scolded. I ran upto him and offered to carry the weight. He was obviously surprised but handed over the bags.

My brother, Sameer, was like the only son my father had. He was good in everything he did, he always had better grades, he was always focused, he was the more understanding types and always ready to sacrifice for me (that was the part I hated the most and the look in my father's eyes when he did such stupid sacrifices). I remember as a kid, someone had gifted him a blue & red engine. I always wanted to play with it but he always placed it beyond my reach on the upper most shelf. When father would be around he would pretend to share his toys and even the new engine and father would pat him fondly. One day, Sameer came tome and offered me the engine, I was an innocent child, and I grabbed it immediately and began playing. Soon after, I heard my father speaking to him, 'So what if Sushant broke your engine, he is your little brother, it's a good thing that you shared it with him. If you score good grades this year, I will buy you a new engine.' He gave me a broken engine and complained that I broke it, he was that kind of a person!

That night, I was lying on the mattress after a hearty dinner, eyes closed and thinking about Suhana, imagining a movie-like setting where a rich girl falls for a poor guy, when I heard my father yell about something and my brother explaining something –

Sameer: I don't understand why Sushant is so jealous of me and why he always damages my things. Today I had offered my bike to him, thinking that these are his days to show off in college, but all he did was spoil it with scratches; even the mirror has been damaged.

Father: Call him, wake him up and get my belt, he needs to be taught a lesson.

Sameer: No father, I will talk to him about this, I am sure he will understand. Please calm down.

Father: You don't have to always support him, this way you are making that loser dependent and good for nothing. He deserves punishment.

Sameer: Maybe what we can do is, cut some of his pocket money and make him repair the scratches.

Father: That sounds reasonable. Why can't he be more like you son? I am sure he won't be there to support me in old-age.

For the first time, I wanted to kill Sameer. What was he trying to prove by this kind of pretense? He never mentioned to father that he had given me the bike to fill petrol and there were absolutely no scratches. He was lying. And I was about to lose my pocket money. Why was Sameer doing this? Anger was boiling within me. I could no longer sleep that night. I had to find a way to deal with this kind of injustice.

The following morning I decided to move out of the house early before anyone could wake up. Luckily, father was out for night shift, so my courage had increased. I wonder why I never connected with my father! If I had to stay out the whole day, I would need some money & I didn't have a penny in my pocket. I thought of picking up a 100 rupee note from Sameer's wallet, he accuses me when I have not done something wrong, so I might as well do something wrong! Sameer was soundly asleep when I woke up around 5.30 am, he faced the wall as he slept and so did my mother. I tiptoed towards the wallet and was surprised to find four 500rupee notes in there as he never carried so much money, rather we could not! I debated with myself heavily before picking up one 500 rupee note. He would obviously know and I would have to face some music when I returned, but I was not bothered. It was half of my pocket money plus he had not returned me the petrol-money too. I stepped out feeling excited, having done something different. I would not spend the entire money, would spend the least and survive on vada-pav the entire day, I thought. After college, I would either take a stroll to Marine drive or while away my time at CST station, but I was sure I would go home as late as possible.

As I sat taking in the breeze at Marine drive, I recollected the events of the day. I did nothing as per the planning. I didn't go to college and I had just 50 bucks in my pocket. I had watched 2 movies, back to back, hogged on chicken biryani at a cheap dhabba along with cheap beer. I realized that if I had to live like this, not caring about the world, I had to earn. I was never interested in studies; I was appearing for Ty. B.com for the 2nd time and had also failed in 12th std. board exams. But I did like something, which I knew my parents could never afford. I wanted to be a movie-star, a hero! I thought of running away from the house with some planning and of course more money! Sameer and I never shared a good equation anyway, so it wouldn't hurt me to dupe him, to con him with some money. I started doing some mental calculations – how much money I would need per month, how I would struggle hard to reach there and how my parents would be finally proud of me once I was famous.

Well, well, I see you are having a great time.

I thought I heard someone; maybe it was some passerby, I thought.

I always thought you were dumb; finally you did something different today.

I looked around. There was a breeze and people were busy with themselves. I started walking towards a chai-wala. I had a cutting chai and sat on the near-by bench.

You can't ignore me, rather I can't ignore you. (A soft laughter)

It was not the first time I had had beer, I knew beer didn't make me hallucinate, maybe I had more than I usually did. I took one more cutting chai and drank it in one shot. I needed to take a drip. I located a public urinal and splashed water on my face. I then unzipped and relieved myself. I examined myself into the dirty mirror to check if I looked sober.

You won't ever look like a star Sushant! (A harsh laughter)

Now I was scared, terribly scared! I was hearing someone's voice, but was not able to see anyone around. I wasn't drunk! But I looked shattered now. I could never go home like this. Mother would know something was wrong and father would torture me with questions. I decided to stay at a friend's place and looked for a booth to inform him about my stay.

The next day I reached home around lunch time. Mother gave me a disapproving look because I was away for a long time, but she was back to being a mother looking at my shabby and hungry state. She fixed up my lunch while I had bath. I was now sure that, that voice was a figment of my imagination. I had not heard it after that, all I could hear was my ever rumbling stomach. I hungrily ate the daal-rice-pickle mother had served. I ate hurriedly with one hand while the other was surfing the TV channel to check the cricket score.

Now that you are feeling better, can we talk?

I almost dropped the remote.

You father is on the way and your mother has found the movie tickets in your pocket. So, before you are grounded and trashed, meet me near the bricked-end of the playground, and I might help you out!

I couldn't move. I sat there froze.

Who are you? I mustered some courage.

No answer. No voice. I got up quickly & found my mother checking my pant pockets & holding the movie tickets, trying to figure out what that piece of paper was. She is not literate enough and she has never been to a movie hall! I moved fast and snatched it from her. I heard her shouting from behind. I looked through the window to find the fat obese figure of my father moving towards the chawl. I put on my chappals and ran towards the playground. I thought I was getting mad, maybe I need some sleep.

Keep moving, don't stop. (The laughter was getting harsher)

I was so scared that I thought my heart would stop beating. I was sweating and shivering at the same time.

I can help you with your problems if you help me with mine. Don't look around because no one can see me. (The laughter was getting meaner). No one can hear me but you can.

My head was spinning, my logic was blurring and my insides were churning. I wanted to puke, I wanted to yell but nothing happened, I could not even breathe! I was suffocating and I finally fainted. I woke up at the same place where I had fainted; I must not have been there for long as it was still bright outside. I hoped that voice was a bad dream.

Wakeywakey.

'Shit. Who the hell are you?' I uttered with panic.

That is what I have been urging to tell you, you weakling! The voice mocked. And I hated *it* instantly. All my life, I had been mocked by people and I was not going to take the same mockery from this insane voice.

I got up angrily and started walking home, determined to ignore *it*.

Hey hey, I have not yet finished. Halt.

'Who the fuck are you to command me like that, you invisible nothing.' I spat angrily. Enough of taking shit from people.

I am a solution to your problems and in return I need a favor too.

'That is not the answer to my question. What are you and why are you talking to me?' I asked irritated.

Look, the answer is straight forward, but a weakling like you will faint again, if I answer it directly. Or worse you may even pee in your pants. (Wicked laughter) Look at yourself, I guess you are about to cry, weakling.

I was breathing heavily, taking in the insult.

You know, your father hates you right...he knows you are good for nothing...

Every word was acting in *its* favor. My temper was boiling. I remembered the times I was being bullied. Anger is what the opponent wants to evoke. I knew that and was trying my best to control it and act sanely.

'I am better off than you, you are not even brave enough to show up, you coward.' I said calmly, weighing each word.

Silence.

'One revolt from me and you run away. You coward!' I was feeling mentally satisfied.

You know I can help you with your problems. (It spoke softly)

I chuckled. 'You need my help more than I need yours, don't you? That is why you have come to me!'

Silence again.

'Come on, now speak up, you invisible coward.'

I..I am a spirit..My name is Sandesh, my friends called me Sandy.

'You are a what?' I asked half afraid and half curious.

You heard me right. I have been trapped between your world and the other side, because I could never cross the barrier.

'Barrier? You mean the one that separates the human and non-human, the living and the dead.' I already had goose bumps as I was speaking this. My fingers were stone cold. Why on earth was this creature speaking to me? I wished this to was a nightmare, I hoped I had not died and this creature was mocking at me, I hoped I had not transferred to some other world.

'Wh..whaat do you want from me?' I had lost my valor along with the color of my face! I was back to being that weakling.

Why, are you scared now? (The mocking tone returning)

'It's but human to react like this. I am alive not dead like you.' I retorted bitterly. 'Why have to come to me, why me, why not someone else?'

I am seeking revenge and I can complete my revenge through you as we have a common enemy.

Enemy? Revenge?

I died because of someone and I need to kill him, so that I can leave this world in peace.

I did not reply, my mind had become numb.

I want you to kill him.

Whaaa..aat? I will never kill someone for your sake...

Think before you say no, killing him will benefit you too

'I am not a murderer, go away, I can't help you.'

I know how much you hate your brother. I hate him too!

Sameer! What did Sameer do to you?

I told you, he killed me.

'He is mean, but he would never kill someone. And...if you say so, go lodge a police complain.' I was never this scared in life before.

Did you forget that I am a spirit! He said with pain.

'I have to go. You are crazy. Go away. I will never help you.' I ran as fast as my footsteps could carry me. I knew Sameer wouldn't kill anyone, but what if he had, what if that *he*was speaking the truth.

Should I confront Sameer? He obviously would never admit, but there had to be some way to find out.

When I reached the door, mother sat crying in the corner and father was searching the locker like a frantic man, as if there was some treasure hidden. Father moved quickly for his weight and was ready to leave with a small red pouch. As far as I remember, father always put away the extra money in that red pouch.

'Can you drop me to Amruta Hospital on the bike? I have to save my only son.' He spoke plainly without looking into my eyes.

'Wha..aat happened, will someone tell me?' I pleaded.

'Sameer has met with an accident and is in the hospital. Now will you ever put yourself to some use! Get me there fast!' father commanded.

'Hospital? What happened?' I asked looking for the bike keys. Father was already descending the stairs, he never bothered to answer.

Wow, it seems my revenge is taken care of. I heard the voice.

As I got on the bike I noticed that there were indeed many scratches and the mirror was broken too. We reached the hospital and found him lying on the bed covered with wounds. He looked at me and my father, smiled meekly. I turned to move away from the scene. Although I didn't like him or my father, I could not bear to witness the scene. I was already laden with guilt. I sat on the bench outside and wanted to speak to *him*.

'You must be very happy now. You had your revenge.' I muttered angrily.

He is still alive, it was a minor accident. The voice was cold.

Father came over to me along with the doctor. 'He has lost a lot of blood.' My father said with voice breaking. 'I hate myself to beg to you but, can you please donate some blood for him.' He spoke, avoiding me in the eyes again.

'Sure father.' I said as humbly as possible. 'I wish I had met with this accident instead of your only son.' I told my father. He looked at me and then avoided my gaze again. As I lay on the adjacent bed, looking at the dripping blood, I wondered what it must be to be like *him,* invisible. My family would surely be happy.

'Would it help if I killed myself instead of you hurting my brother? I asked *him.* 'Maybe I was wrong, I need your help too.'

You don't care for your life because you are not aware of this pain and misery of living like this. All alone, lost in the dark world, suffering!

'Can we exchange lives, like they show in movies?'

'Are you talking alone?' Sameer's feeble voice interrupted.

'No..no..just blabbering! How..how are you feeling?' I asked, not that I really wanted to know.

'I want to confess something before father comes here.' Sameer spoke softly.

'Yes, of course…there is a long list of confessions you need to make…the recent one being the lie about the bike!' I blurted out angrily.

'I am sorry about that, I was scared. But there is something more..something I am ashamed off.'

I frowned. *Here comes the truth.*

'I hit someone yesterday. I was so scared that I did not even turn back.'

'Whaat! You…'

'There is something more. I saw his body lying is the opposite room, he seems to be in coma.'

My body. In coma. Which means there is a chance I can still live. There was a mixture of emotions in his voice.

'Can you take me to him, I want to apologize…'

'Apologize…You killed someone!!' Everything was happening so fast, I could hardly react.

'I can't live with the burden anymore. What if I die pertaining to these injuries without saying sorry?'

'You left someone to die and all you care about is your burden of guilt. What if you had not seen him in this hospital, you would have lived on, guilt-free! I never liked you Sameer, you very well know why, but I never knew you were a coward.'

'You are right, I will confess everything to father if I get well and stay alive. With death standing on my head, I have realized I was always mean. God has punished me with this accident, I may never be able to walk again! Before anything worse happens please take me to him and his family.'

'You think saying sorry will help, you think you can reverse the damage you have done?'

'Please Sushant. Please do me this favor.'

I carried Sameer on the wheel chair to the opposite room where Sandy's body lay – calm and serene. His mother sat by his bed sobbing.

I knew Sameer would back out, so I spoke up before he changed his mind.

'How is Sandesh, aunty? Do not worry, a friend of mine is a very good doctor, I am sure he will help him recover.' I lied. 'Aunty, this is my brother Sameer and he has come to apologize for this accident. He is responsible for this.'

A wave of shock crossed her face and she started accusing us. The nurse came by and asked us to leave.

Why are you fighting for me? Came the voice, soft and calm.

'I am standing up for something I should have done long before, standing up for myself. I will pray with all my heart and hope that you recover soon and maybe we can be good friends.' I heard a faint smile.

Whatever I told you in the playground was all made up, except the revenge part, but not anymore, I mean revenge won't help, besides God has his ways of punishing the wrong doers. I have been lying here for close to 48 hours only but in this form it felt like days. It's painful like this.

'Who are you talking to' Sameer asked.

'Forget it, you won't understand.'

'How did you know his name was Sandesh?'

I was amused by his curiosity and pleased by his ignorance. 'It's beyond your scope to understand Sameer.'

You are right, that is why, only you could hear me. Sandesh interrupted.

'But how did you find me? I asked Sandesh, leaving Sameer baffled as to who I was talking to. I gestured the nurse to take him inside his room so that I could continue with my conversation.

The accident happened exactly at the same signal, where you dropped off that girl. I recognized the bike immediately but I had a vague idea of how the biker looked at the night of the accident. I was not sure it was you so I followed you home, I recognized Sameer from his moustache and his checkered clothing. I yelled at him and questioned him but it didn't work. The strain in you relation with your brother and father made me come up with this plan – needless to say that you were the only one who could hear me. Sorry for all that trouble…I am…

I waited for a while, for him to speak.

'Sandesh? Are you here?'

There was a hustle of footsteps and the nurse informing the doctor – The patient in coma is responding.

I rushed to the room and found Sandesh moving his fingers and slowly his eyes. His mother was too happy to notice my presence. I was happy that he would be back to normal. I tried to fix my gaze on him hoping he would recognize but he gave me a blank look and closed his eyes again. His mother panicked and I heard *him*.

Thank you friend! I came back to tell you this. I may not recognize you or even remember any of this once I go back to the human world; and I guess but you will be locked in my sub conscious memory for ever... maybe I can recognize you, if we meet in the next birth.

Sandesh opened his eyes once again and looked at me blankly. I smiled at myself and life's strange ways.

Quite a few things changed after that – changed for the good. Sameer confessed many of his misdoings and that changed the way my father treated me. We are not enemies now, to call us friends would be stretching it. Sameer is recovering and is able to stand on his feet.

I cleared my TY exam and got myself a job. Someday I wish to take up an acting course too!

Mihir Shah

Belonging to the city of dreams, Mumbai, Mihir Shah is a 28 year old is a happy go fellow; ready to take on the world with his charming persona and never say die attitude. He has contributed to anthologies by Sanmati Publishers and Half Baked Beans Publishers.

An interior designer by force, a business man by choice, a singer by heart and a writer by chance, Mihir graduated from the Rachana Sansad College of Interior Designing to handle his glass business by expertise. His motto in life is - 'Give respect, take respect'.

You can reach him at - www.facebook.com/mihir.shah.9659.

Neoni D'Souza

NeoniD'souza, 23 years, is quite simple but affable girl, born in Ankeshwar, Gujarat. She has completed her Bachelor's in Information Technology from Srinivas Institute of Technology, Karnataka. Currently, she is working with one of the leading software solution company, designated at Quality Analyst.

Being a technocrat, she has a deep affection for literary. She loves reading, cooking, gardening, handcrafting, travelling and currently trying her hands on playing guitar. She has been a contributing author for 'Syahi – The Power of Pen', 'Tere hi Liye', 'A Night in Paradise' and 'Myraid Tales'.

You can reach her at: neonidsouza@gmail.com

Facebook connect: https://www.facebook.com/neoni23

15

AN ETERNAL CRUSH

Mihir Shah & Neoni D'souza

It was a lazy afternoon with a chilly climate, when I was returned from my college. Little did I know that when I would reach home, I would be alone at home?

'Ting tong...Ting tong' I again rang the bell, but mom didn't open the door. I rang my neighbor's doorbell, asked for the spare key and entered the house.

The moment I stepped in, I looked for mom thinking that she must be sleeping in her room. I entered her room, but it was empty. I went into the kitchen and there was a note by mom stuck on the fridge.

"Hey *beta*, I had to go urgently to meet your *masi*. I will be back by 7pm. Love you".

I was a little angry at her for not being around to do my daily chores. I went to my room, threw my bag on the bed and changed into my shorts. I took my lunch from the kitchen and glued myself to the sofa. I was surfing the channels, but there wasn't anything interesting to watch so switched to *Cartoon Network*.

I remember watching cartoons as a kid. As I grew up my taste changed and became mature. But who said mature people don't watch cartoons. I was watching Tom & Jerry, though I had seen it repeatedly. But I started to lose interest as soon as I finished my lunch. I was bored to death so chose to sleep as I was very tired.

After what seemed like few hours of sleep, I woke up.

'What the#^%$"!!??'

I looked at my watch and realized that I had just slept for half an hour. I guessed this afternoon was going to be the most boring day of my life. Even sleep left me alone! I was still lying on the bed and was searching for my mobile. It was right below me. My mom says that when I sleep, I try almost all possible positions of sleeping. I sleep with my head on the upper side of the bed and when I wake up, I am upside down.

I checked my phone. 'Six missed calls. Oh god, Khyati will kill me.' I said to myself.

"Hey Khyati! Hi!" I murmured in a sleepy tone.

"Where the hell have you been?" Khyati sounded pissed.

"Nothing sweetie, I slept with the phone below me so I couldn't even feel the vibration. I slept immediately after getting back from college. I didn't even have my lunch. You know, sweetheart, today's practical and lectures were so tiring." I lied and sounded like a sweet puppy.

It's really necessary to lie when you are in a relationship. It's my personal advice. No offense to reader.

"Don't you forget, Manan, we are catching up tonight for a movie." she commanded.

"Yes, my love, I promise." I was always a sweet liar.

Actually, I never loved Khyati truly. She was just a crush to me. I was with her just because she was one of the most gorgeous girls in our college and I wanted other boys to feel jealous about me.

Well, I was still wondering what to do after I hung up the phone. This was indeed one of the most boring days. I got up and took out the laptop from my bag. I logged into *Facebook*. Well, my friends-list was increasing day by day. It was 2000+ and all credit went to the fact that I had a gorgeous girlfriend. Many friends including Khyati were online. Just to get rid of her boring lovey-dovey talks I chose to be in offline mode.

I saw Rohit online too. I buzzed him and chatted with him for half an hour. We chatted about sexy bitches, sports & of course *KHYATI*. Well, that half an hour was just hilarious. Suddenly the lazy afternoon turned into laughter riot. But as you know, boy to boy talk is not lengthy as girl to girl gossips!

I logged out and went into the kitchen for a grab as I was famished again. When mom is not around I really get confused not knowing what is kept where and miss her nagging. But then Khyati makes up for it with her forever ranting comments and suggestions – *Manan, don't do this! Manan, don't do that! Manan, wear smarter clothes!Manan, switch off the TV and complete your projects! Manan, don't talk to other girls! Manan, you love me no? Manan, you miss me no?*

'Urgh! Women, are always nagging, no matter the age,' I grimaced, as I indulged into a spicy packet of chips and grappled to finish my college assignment.

It took me almost 2 hrs to complete my project and I felt that I was going to top in my class. After completing the work, I again switched on to my laptop. I logged on to Facebook and Yahoo messenger again.

Social networking sites are like the fridge; even after knowing there is nothing in there, you still want to open it again and again.

'Oh god, Khyati was still online. Gosh, this chick is crazy. God knows what she gossips about. She doesn't have any work on the earth. Such a silly bimbo!' This time I chose to go online and the moment it showed a green dot, Khyati pinged me.

"Hi babyyy, how are you?" she messaged instantly. I wasn't a mean guy, so I replied. I was always a woman charmer. Though I look geek and unappealing, my plus point is my way of talking. I always use sweet, poisonous words on my prey and that's how I proposed to Khyati and made her my girlfriend.

"Hey cutie, I am good. How is my baby doing?" I asked with those sweet words.

"You know what Manan, I was chatting with Shonali and she was bitching about her boyfriend. I felt so bad for him. I just hope you aren't doing that to me? I hope you are not bitching about me to Rohit?"

I was frozen. I thought Khyati came to know that I do bitch about her.

"No, my cuchie puchie. You think I will ever do that to you? My Khyati is the most gorgeous of all and I cannot even think of hurting her." my lying skills excelled.

"Awww...I love you Manan." she purred.

"I love you too baby. Bye... *mwaaah*".

After that proud moment of lie, I rolled myself in bed naughtily and got lost in my thoughts.

***

'Buzz. Buzz. Buzz'

I suddenly got up from bed listening to that buzzer from my Yahoo Messenger chat.

Chat: 'คุณเป็นอย่างไรบ้าง'

A window popped up in my messenger. I could not understand which language it was. It was weird. I immediately opened Google translator and typed this message. It said "How are you". It was Thai language. I replied to that chat using the same translator.

Me: ผมชั้นดี (I am fine)

Chat: คุณมาจากที่ไหน

Me: Hey I am sorry, but I don't understand this language. I replied your previous question by using a translator.

Chat: Oh, I am sorry.

Me: It's ok. No problem. What's your name?

Chat: I am Suwaluck. Where are you from?

Me: I am from Mumbai, India. Where are you from?

Suwaluck: I am from Krabi, Thailand.

I immediately opened a new tab in chrome and typed Thailand and clicked on its Wikipedia.

M: Oh, Thailand, great. It's also called 'Land of the free'.

S: Yes. How you know?

M: I know a very little about Thailand. (I lied again. Google rocks!)

S: What's your name?

M: My name is Manan, and I am 17yr.

S: Oh, 17yr. I am 28.

***

'Ting-tong' 'ting-tong', the doorbell rang, disturbing me.

"Hey mom, how come you returned early?" I asked her with an irritated tone.

"Why, should I ask your permission before coming?" she replied sensing something wrong.

"What took so much time to open the door, Manan?" she questioned like a CBI official.

"Ah.. Ummmm.. No nothing mom. I was sleeping. How's *Masi*?" I pretended to be a sweet kid.

"Yea, she is fine. She wanted some help for Ishika's wedding." she replied.

I mumbled something disinterestedly and immediately ran in my room and switched off the laptop.

"Hope you had your lunch Manan? Are you done with your studies? Did you clean your room?" mom was yelling from the kitchen.

"Yes Mom. I finished my lunch, my assignments, cleaned my room, put my dirty clothes in the machine; now I am all set and am going for movie with friends." I said in one breath. I slammed the door and left for the movie.

Though I didn't have a license, driving was one of my passions and I used to go for long drives every night with my friends and had also landed myself in trouble many times. But as they say *'Money is everything you need'* and bribing is the best way to get rid of your problems.

Khyati was waiting for me, but I was spared by her nagging as I managed to reach the movie hall on time. It was an action movie which I loved watching but Khyati always hated them. So she was constantly talking to me during the movie and even chatted on the phone. Sometimes she tried to get naughty which I loved, but nothing comes between me and action movies!

"Phewww. Finally, it's over. Huh." Khyati taunted.

"Oh my baby, you know how much I love action movies, now let's go."

Soon we reached the parking lot. Not seeing many cars, I tried getting a little naughty with her.

"Stop it Manan, it's the parking area. Somebody will see." Khyati stopped me. (*Oh god..!! Why are these girls so dumb? They can get naughty and want to hold your hand in the movie hall when it's filled with people, but don't allow you to kiss when there is no one to watch)*

"No baby, you can't stop me from kissing you and grabbing you in my arms."

I pulled Khyati towards me and held her face between my palms. Her breath paced. I swayed the strand of hair which covered her face and gently placed my lips on hers. Her emotions were high and she wanted more of it. She immediately opened her lips and let her tongue meet mine. Our tongues started rolling into each other. We got into the car; I pulled back the co-driver seat and laid her down gently. I could feel her minty breath on my face. I kissed her thighs which were semi covered with her hot black shorts. Her fair skin was all the more inviting. I started exploring her body and kissed aggressively. I let my hand go inside her Tee and started pressing her breast tenderly, which made her go crazy. She moaned loudly exciting me but before I could respond with equal zeal, I heard a knock on my car door.

"Sir, it's too late and I am afraid that you have to move your car out." said the security guard with a sad tone after witnessing the entire scene. I gave him a 500 rupee note and winked at him, he accepted it greedily. We left from there reluctantly, cursing my luck. After dropping Khyati to her place, I headed back home and slept off.

Next morning, I don't know, how long that ray of sunlight had been peeking through the gap in the curtains before it found its way onto my face; nor do I know how long it took me to become aware of it. I'd been dreaming that I was flying a plane, which is strange, because I never had any ambition of being a pilot. It felt great to be up there above the sunlit clouds, seeing the green countryside through the occasional gap. I fought to ignore that errant sunbeam, to get back to my dream, but the moment had passed. I heard my neighbor's SUV rolling down his drive, and somewhere a dog barked. I rubbed my knuckles into my eyes to drive away the sleep.

I got fresh and logged into Facebook and Yahoo messenger.

***

'Buzz' 'Buzz' 'Buzz' 'Buzz'

Omg! There were so many pings from Suwaluck. I had totally forgotten about chatting with this lady.

I immediately replied her and thank god she was online too.

M: อรุณสวัสดิ์ (good morning)

S: Oh! Buddha. He learned Thai so fast.

M: Hahahaha. How are you?

S: I am good.

M: So what do you do?

S: I have my own set up of computers and so I am online most of the time. What do you do?

M: I am studying in the 3rd year of commerce.

We started knowing about each other's life; likes, dislikes, hobbies, etc. I started spending lot of time on Yahoo and wanted to know more and more about her. This had become my daily routine. Wake up & chat, chat, before lunch, chat after lunch, chat before dinner, chat post dinner, chat before sleeping!

I felt I had become half Thai and she had become half Indian. I had started calling her princess. From day one, I never had any intention of flirting with her. I never made her feel awkward or embarrassed her with my silly questions. For a moment I felt I had grown up and was acting like a 28yr old guy. *Sometimes it takes ages to know someone and sometimes all you need is a small chat.* Soon we exchanged our numbers and I called her from the free 'LINE' software. We kept calling each other and in a few months we became very good friends.

It was 27th December when I told her about my birthday being on 1st January.

She was excited about it. All this while I had started ignoring Khyati deliberately and spend more time at home, chatting with Suwaluck. Although I didn't care about Khyati I knew how to handle girls very well.

Suwaluck was planning something for me on my birthday as she had started asking me to share my childhood pictures and things related to where I lived. She had some magical spell that was drawing me towards her, an unknown force of attraction towards her in spite of the age difference and the geographic barrier between us. I used to act as if I was totally unaware about her plans for me. I loved that feeling that someone is making efforts to make me feel special. I didn't understand whether it was just an infatuation or love that I had begun to feel for her.

***

1st January, 12:00 am. My birthday.

I was in my world of dreams when I got a call. I jumped up to pick up the call, but whole excitement level dimmed when I found that the caller was Khyati and not Suwaluck. I didn't want to take the call, but I also didn't want to break someone's heart, especially Khyati's, as somewhere I was keeping her in a blind room of love!

"Hi baby, Happy Birthday and Happyy New Yearrrrrr!" Khyati shouted.

"Hello, thank you so much, love." I acted to be happy.

"There will be a surprise for you tomorrow, are you ready?" Khyati questioned.

"Hmm, ok sweetie. Hey listen, mom & dad are knocking the door. I will call you back in the morning" I lied.

My phone was buzzing every minute after I disconnected Khyati's call, but every time I looked at my cell it was some or the other friend, but not Suwaluck. I didn't know what went wrong that she didn't even call to wish me. I was upset, I tried calling her once but her phone was not reachable. I threw my phone in anger and went off to sleep.

It was the first day of the New Year and my birthday too, but I didn't have any excitement and was lying on bed like a wooden log. Suddenly there was a knock on my bedroom door. It was mom. I didn't want to wake up nor wanted anybody to wish me.

"*Beta*, get up. Are you alright? Why on earth are you locked up in the room on your birthday? See you havegot gifts and a bouquet of flowers." mom said.

'Oh shit, this Khyati. Why does she need to do these things? Now what will I answer mom, if she enquires about Khyati?' I murmured to myself.

"Who is this Suwaluck, *beta*?" mom asked from the living room.

I jumped off the bed in excitement, my happiness didn't have any limits.

"Mom please don't touch or open anything." I warned mom, running to the living room.

Mom smiled at me and went about her chores. No matter how I spoke to her, I was always her favorite, spoilt brat especially on my birthday.

There was a huge bouquet of white orchids; my favorite. There was also a note on it. *Meet me at Hyatt Regency hotel. See you at 10 am.*

I was jumping with joy, I could finally meet Suwaluck. I had decided to express my feelings to her without even thinking of her reaction.

I looked at my watch 'Oh shit, its 9:30 am, I need to rush soon.'

I just hopped in my best clothes and was on my way.

Many thoughts were running through my mind –

We had spent countless hours just talking through a phone or through a chat. We had not even seen each other. But then, we had learned to trust, to sacrifice, and lose a bit of sleep due the time difference but we had learned to cherish every single moment. Now, when I have got this chance to see her it felt like of the best feelings in the world. I was waiting for this moment, which I thought would never come. But now it had come at a right time and I would want to cherish it forever.

Finally, I reached the destination. She was waiting at the reception. I had never seen such a beautiful woman ever. I was mesmerized by her beauty. She saw me and hugged me. Her smile conveyed happiness.

"Come, let's go, I will take you to my favorite place." I said. We both were silent on our way towards Nariman point. I took her to my favorite restaurant 'Relish'. After having a delicious meal, we both went for a short walk near Marine Drive.

"Here, it is something for you." Suwaluck took out a beautifully wrapped gift from her hand bag.

I couldn't wait to open it. I was shocked to see that it was a beautiful photo album and most importantly it was handmade. I had never ever cried in my life, but this was something special which made me emotional. Every page described me so perfectly. She had covered all the moments in my life including Khyati, about whom I had told Suwaluck.

"Thank you so much. This is the best gift I could get. It really means a lot to me, Suwaluck," I said holding her hands, "I loved your gift, thank you so much for coming. You made my day special by your presence. Why did you come all the way along? Why did you take so much trouble? You are new to this place, I would have made all the arrangements for you." I asked her.

"I just wanted to see you happy. There is a reason behind my visit, Manan. I want to tell you something which you should know about me." Suwaluck had a serious look on her face.

"Yes, I am all ears." I said, a bit nervous.

"Please don't be mad at me. Listen to me carefully." Suwaluck reassured holding my hands.

"Manan, you are very nice guy. I have been chatting and talking with you since a couple of months and I have judged that you are not the type you portray to people. You are a very caring and sane guy." I was confused as to why Suwaluck was talking all this.

"Manan, I am not going to live long. I have brain tumor which is in its initial stage. I still travelled and took the risk of meeting you. I knew you have started developing feelings for me, so I wanted to stop you before it was too late." Suwaluck said and my world was devastated listening to this.

"Manan, your feelings for me are temporary, like a crush. Khyati is a very nice girl, you should appreciate her love for you. Promise me that you will never leave her." Suwaluck continued.

I didn't want to agree to her but I still nodded. I was just confused as to how to react at this.

"I just wanted to take away some memories of you, so I visited India. I have come all the way because I also have feelings for you but we are not meant to be together, you know that Manan. Our age difference, cultures and moreover my disease will always part us. I do love you Manan, but Khyati is the woman for you, not I." Suwaluck said, with utmost love in her eyes.

"But why didn't you tell me all this before?" I asked, frustrated.

"Manan, I knew you would fall apart, so I wanted to show you the right path." she said.

"Turn back, there is a surprise for you." she added with an exciting gleam in her eyes.

I turned back to find Khyati.

'Wooooo…. that's another shock now.' These were the words that slipped from my mouth.

"How do you both know each other?" I questioned in shock.

"Manan, I and Khyati got to know each other through Facebook. Every time you had been telling me how much you hate her childish nature, her constant nagging, you also unknowingly happened to mention, how much you care for her. She may not be your true love, but she's definitely not any passing-by crush, I am convinced of that." Suwaluck continued, "Your mom knows about my visit and she also knows about Khyati".

I got another big shock. I think it was a '*shock day*' rather than my '*birth day*'.

"You brought us together, Manan. We both love you and want you to be happy." said Khyati coming close to me. Her tone suddenly sounded mature and understanding.

"When Suwaluck came to know about her disease, she didn't want you to suffer so she connected with me through Facebook and told me everything about your virtual relation and she also told me what you feel about me." Khyati's tone was a little low for a second but bubbly the next when she said, "But Suwaluck knew that no matter how much you try to fake, you always cared for me and somewhere loved me but you didn't realize it. She wanted you to realize that, so I helped her to come to India".

I was just shocked and felt shattered that I was so selfish about Khyati all along. She did all this for me and I never took her love seriously.

"I am always with you, don't worry" Khyati came and hugged me. "I am sorry Manan; as all this while I suffocated you in this relationship. I will try my level best to give you all possible happiness." Khyati kissed me on my cheeks.

I could feel the sun setting far away and its subtle light fell on Khyati's beautiful cheeks. She was blushing or maybe I only saw her with a new realization in my heart.

It was like the best day for me. I got my crush, Khyati back with all her deep love and I also got a best friend, Suwaluck. I was very afraid of losing Suwaluck, but fate brought us altogether.

The day was about to end.

"Happy birthday once again, Manan." said Khyati & Suwaluck in unison and they both kissed my cheeks. I was on cloud nine. I hugged both of them.

Later we all went to Suwaluck's hotel to drop her. She was packing her luggage and was ready to go back to Thailand. She had come for a day trip to make me happy and make my birthday special.

Suwaluck had tears in her eyes as we all reached the airport. She had the most memorable time in India. Once again we all had a group hug. Suwaluck kissed my forehead and entered the airport. We waved at her till she disappeared.

***

It's been a decade now. Khyati and I are happily married. We are very much in contact with Suwaluck. In fact our honeymoon destination was Thailand. It's indeed a beautiful place. Now Suwaluck's health has improved with all the medication and therapy. She has also got married to a Thai – American guy named Jimmy.

Though we (Suwaluck and I) both grew beyond our infatuation phase for each other and married people who loved us dearly, yet we hold a fond place for each other in our hearts. A place of respect and affection, something none can replace. I will always be thankful to Suwaluck for making me grow up, realize my mistake of ignoring Khyati's love and for making my crush, my life.

I love you Khyati, truly. I said to myself.

But, Suwaluck will always be in a corner of my heart as my long distant crush. An eternal crush that showed me the path towards my true love, Khyati.

Thanks for Reading